Michael O'F

GW01458554

When They Followed Henry Joy

RIPOSTE BOOKS DUBLIN

First Published in 1997 by

RIPOSTE BOOKS

28 Emmet Rd Dublin 8. Ireland

Cover by the author.
Printed by DOCUPRINT Dublin

ISBN 1 901596 00 1

Contents

Dublin at the end of the 18th century.

Introduction

From my earliest schooldays I have always enjoyed hearing about, and reading about the Rebellion of '98. In no other period of Irish history are so many heroic figures and illustrious names crammed into such a short space of time. Each of these great characters is worthy of a biography exclusively to himself and many such excellent biographies have already been written. However, I have been disappointed when reading these biographies to find their subjects are treated somewhat in isolation from their counterparts in that great age. In this way, when I read about Wolfe Tone, I find barely a mention of HenryJoy McCracken, when I read about HenryJoy, I find barely a mention of Lord Edward and when I read about Lord Edward, I find no mention of James Hope. Needless to say, Wexford must have been in Australia when some of these biographies were written. In bringing together the elements of this book, I have tried to correlate all the events so as to give some kind of a real time picture of events which were highly contemporaneous but which are so often treated in isolation. To achieve this, I felt obliged to strike a balance between omitting some of the more entertaining trivia in order to avoid digressing too far from the central theme, i.e. The Rebellion of '98, and at the same time supplying the necessary details to explain the actions of the principal characters and the reasons for their successes and their failures. I myself am constantly surprised at how feasible the whole rebellion was, for in no subsequent era could any leader claim, as Lord Edward did, that he had a quarter of a million United Irishmen ready to follow his lead. Of course there are no new facts in this book and much of the information has been published on numerous previous occasions and some quite recently. However the minor overlooked piece makes a jigsaw complete and when all the pieces are in view, the whole is seen anew.

Acknowledgements

The information in this book has been gathered from many sources, old and new and over a number of years. I would like to express my sincere gratitude to the Staffs of the National Library of Ireland, The Linen Hall Library Belfast, The Belfast Library, The Gilbert Library, The Ulster Museum, Trinity College Library and Trinity College Manuscript Library, The British National Library and The Dublin Civic Museum for their assistance during my research for this book.

Illustrations curtsey The National Library Of Ireland, The Linen Hall Library, Belfast and The Betjemen Library.

This book is dedicated solely to the memory of
Henry Joy McCracken

James
Hope

James Hope

James Hope 1764-1847

It was said of James Hope and his relationship to the United Irish Society that;

*" He watched over its cradle and walked after its hearse. "*1

It would be foolish to try to understand, read or study the events of 1798 without first considering the life and actions of one James Hope. He was 83 years old when he died in 1847 and it is due to his longevity that we have a detailed account of the events of that time.

He had the closest possible acquaintance with HenryJoy McCracken, with Samuel Neilson, with Thomas Russell and with Robert Emmet. He also had regular contact with Lord Edward Fitzgerald and many of the other members of the Leinster Directory, as he was an emissary between Dublin and Belfast from 1795 until 1803.

An examination of Hope's itinerary for 1796 will give some idea of his importance to the society of the United Irishmen and of the extent of his knowledge and contacts within that organisation.

	Miles
Belfast to Roscommon	100
Roscommon to Belfast	100
Belfast to Dublin	80
Dublin to Prosperous	15
Prosperous to Dublin	15
Dublin to Roscommon	79
Roscommon to Dublin	79
Dublin to Startford	26
Startford to Dublin	26
Lost in Wicklow	18
Dublin to Roscommon	79
Roscommon to Belfast	100

Hope had to cross the Shannon at Athlone and this increased the length of his journey from Roscommon to Belfast. He did not travel by express but made numerous stops along the way. Together with his associates such as Daniel Digney, Richard Dry and William McCabe, Hope was involved in the establishment of United Irish Societies in Castleblaney, Roscommon Strokestown, Ballyhayes, Butlersbridge, Newtownhamilton, Enniskillen, Ballynamore, Cashcarringon, Carrick-on-Shannon, Tulamore as well as Wicklow and Dublin.

In a letter to Dr. Madden written in 1843 James Hope gave advice to any one interested in the history of the 1798 period.

" To write the history of Ireland from 1798 to 1804 is a difficult task. Many useful documents are missing and only a few are still alive who have a true knowledge of the events of that period. The power and ingenuity of our enemies in suppressing and distorting the truth has never been surpassed in any age.

When writing of Ulster you will require an extensive view of the influence with which the patriots had to contend- sectarian, mercantile and landed interests, greater than in any other part of Ireland. The other provinces had only the landed and church interests against them; our landed aristocracy extended to the forty shilling freeholder, a class hardly known in the rest of Ireland, We also had the manufacturing aristocracy, little known in the south and corruption ran through all of these different channels.

To contradict falsehood was called "sedition" in the wicked times of Pitt and Castlereagh and as a result the work of the historian is very difficult.

Neilson, McCracken , Russell and Robert Emmet were the leading men in that struggle and men with whom I had the closest intimacy. They were men, Irishmen of whom I met none more true and none could be more true. The cause of Ireland was then confined to a few individuals. The masses had no idea of the possibility of managing their own affairs. It is easy to asperse our struggle, we had bad men amongst us, but no good cause requires the support of bad men. The bad men who joined us had to play the hypocrite; they had the enemies ranks to retreat to and whenever they feared detection they charged us with their own evil intentions. I was a bosom friend of Neilson, McCracken,

Russell and Robert Emmet, I mean there was not a thought regarding public affairs that one of us would conceal from the other and for their truth I would answer with my life. Volumes have been written recording the crimes of mankind, but the causes from which they spring is often overlooked. If the historians would only state what they know to be the facts, truth would run in a freer channel from age to age. From the extension of literature the present age lies under a heavier responsibility than any other for the transmission of the truth to posterity. "2

signed   *JAMES HOPE 1843.*

James Hope was born in Templepatrick in 1764. His grandfather was a highland refugee who was buried at Mallusk. The family were Presbyterians and he remembered being subjected to bigoted sermons on the Sabbath from a very early age. He remembered that there were only two Catholic families, named Neill and Tolan, in Templepatrick all the other natives had been cleared out. He also remembered regiments of Protestants setting off to fight in the American war of Independence in 1776. When the British had difficulty in gaining recruits to put down the American rebellion, Lord Hillsborough said " discourage the linen trade and you will have soldiers." When this was done nearly 5000 Protestants went off to fight in America. Also at this time George III wanted to use German troops to maintain order in Ireland, but the Protestants all over Ireland resisted this plan and set-up their own Volunteers.

James Hope spent thirteen weeks at school before he started work as a mechanic in Templepatrick. Luckily for him his new employers took an interest in furthering his education and he learned to read and write with their help in his spare time. He also spent some time working as a farm labourer before serving a full apprenticeship to the linen trade. Later he married his employer 's daughter, Rose Mullin and they had four children. James Hope's political involvement began in 1790 when he joined the Roughford Corps of the Volunteers. That same year the Belfast Battalion of the volunteers celebrated the taking of the Bastille on the 14th of July. The following year the battalion he belonged to marched out in coloured clothes with green cockades and a banner which read;

"Our Gallic brother was born July 14th 1789,
*Alas, we are still in embryo."*3

James Hope joined the United Irishmen on the 26th of June 1795. He says that members were chosen by ballot. He was proposed and approved and had to take a test. He says that he could have declined to take the test, but would have been obliged to keep secret the contents of the test. He agreed to take it but was sad that their objectives could not have been pursued by more open means. He joined at Hightown but later moved to Mallusk. The society was mostly composed by men from the Volunteers. He was appointed to the Baronial Committee of Belfast and there he met HenryJoy McCracken for the first time.

Hope was never a great public speaker but was more effective meeting people in small groups. He described his mind as being like Swift's Church, " *the more there was inside, the slower the mass came out .* " He joined the United Irishmen to promote the objectives of the Volunteers, it was only later that he became a radical.

Hope was active in 1796, 1797, 1798 and again in 1803 alongside Robert Emmet. He mainly functioned as an emissary, travelling from place to place, organising people and carrying messages. He took orders from Russell, Neilson and McCracken and communicated with people whom he had sworn never to name, but all of whom were in close confidence with the Directory. He was a delegate to the County Committee, in the confidence of the Ulster Directory, and in the confidence of the principal members of the Leinster Directory.

Hope maintains that the reasons for the Revolution of 1798 are greatly misunderstood. He points out that the manufacturers and industrialists in the North were accumulating new wealth. Their offspring were more skilled and could save money. They often rented cottages from the Catholic farmers and were then able to offer higher rents to the Landlords at the end of the farmers tenure. This created ill-will between the farmers and the traders and those with the new skills. Roman Catholic tenant farmers were being forced off their holdings because others could afford higher rents for their land . The Catholics joined together in bands called the Defenders. These in turn were then opposed by the Peep-o-day boys.

Samuel Neilson and Luke Teeling, a Catholic linen merchant had the idea of forming a union between the United Irishmen and the Defenders. While Neilson and McCracken were organising the United Irishmen in Belfast, Charles Teeling worked hard to unite the Catholics and Defenders in all the small towns of Ulster. Through his efforts even the Peep-O-Day boys and the Defenders were made friends and sworn in the Brotherhood of the United Irishmen. However it was HenryJoy McCracken who organised that body of men, 7000 strong, most of them formerly Defenders which was ready for the rising of 1798.

Hope maintained that while the system in the South was corrupt the system in the North was even more corrupt.
" *Belfast was the most corrupt town on the face of the earth. Besides the interests of the Churchlords and the Landlords, there were the interests of Manufacturing and Commerce, of Fictitious Capital, Fictitious credit and Fictitious Titles. On top of this you had a state-funded Clergy propagating bigotry from the pulpits. Both the Pulpit and the Law were completely controlled by the Aristocracy. Aristocratic Monetary Influence was so complete that only its own corruption could destroy it. Power was Law and Physical force settled every question.* "

Hope went further and said that ;

"*There are circumstances which should never be forgotten in relation to 1798. The people were excluded from any say in the framing of the laws by which they were governed. The higher ranks usurped this right as well as many other rights, by force, by fraud and by lies. It was by force that the poor were subdued*

11

*and dispossessed of their land and by fiction that the titles of the spoilers were established. "*4

Observing the Orange Order which was set-up in 1795, Hope said that it was first composed of "Yeomen, renegade croppies, hangers on around landlords, lower order clergymen with their spies and informers, together with the bullies of the market place." *"These renegades caused more bloodshed in 1798 than the open enemy whom we knew and could avoid."*

Hope said that in every district there were men who had become so used to swearing contradictory oaths that they would swear to anything. And there was money to be made from swearing the way the Bench wanted.

Throughout 1795 and early 1796 the influence of the united Irishmen began to be felt at all the public places across the north. At fairs, markets and social meetings, the ideas of the United Irishmen began to gain ground. There was less strife and quarrelling and even less drunkenness. The Peep-O-Day Boys and the Defenders made peace with each other and for a while Ulster seemed like a united family. A delegation was sent to Dublin to disseminate the views among the working class.

James Hope and John Metcalfe comprised that delegation and for a while Hope lived in Balbriggan where he worked for a Protestant silk weaver. From there he travelled to Dublin to carry on the business of the Society. Later he moved to the Liberties to avoid detection. He was able to obtain work and accommodation there and it made it easier to carry out his work for the United Irishmen. Within a short time Hope returned to the North to report success but was quickly sent back again to carry on further work. He then brought his family to Dublin where they remained for a further ten years.

From Dublin the Society soon spread to other counties and to the other provinces. A national committee was formed which met in Dublin. The leaders of the United Irishmen were still unknown to the general membership, for members only knew the members of their own local society except for delegates to the higher levels.

When Hope returned to Dublin he again got to work in the Liberties and the United Irish Societies were soon spread throughout the city. Hope was still operating in conjunction with his friend Metcalfe. They were entrusted with information which was leaked and Hope came under suspicion. A meeting was arranged and the two men were summoned to attend at a venue on the Sth. Circular road near the Grand Canal. Six men were instructed to meet Hope and his friend and drown them. However the six had gone for a few drinks and forgotten to leave the pub in time. Hope and Metcalfe turned up for the meeting but went home when it got dark. Hope only discovered what it was all about when his employer was surprised to see him still alive the following morning! On a previous occasion while working with Neilson, Russell and McCracken in Belfast, an Orangeman had offered Hope £500 if he would provide information to convict them. He agreed to meet the man (Ferris Martin) at a certain tavern. Meanwhile Hope arranged for Neilson, Russell, and McCracken to be hidden in another room. When Martin appeared they all confronted him and forced him to reveal who was putting up the money. McCracken was highly delighted with this piece of counter espionage. However McCracken was totally opposed to action being taken against informers.

Hope continued to live, work and organise in the Liberties throughout 1797 during which time he visited Neilson and McCracken in Kilmainham and Russell who was held in Newgate. He also made occasional visits to Belfast where he witnessed a deterioration in conditions there due to the activities of General Lake. He found that more and more of his former comrades were held in prison and besides the information being obtained through spies and informers, the Government was now getting information through the use of torture. He also noticed that many who had previously shown great interest in the cause of Unity were now being frightened away by repression. Although the province of Ulster had been first prepared and best prepared for the rising of 1798 the enthusiasm and energy shown in '95 and '96 had begun to dissipate by 1797. Their leaders McCracken, Russell and Neilson were all in prison in the south. Even James Hope was living in Dublin. The repression during 1797 might have induced the population to rebel if their

13

leadership were present. In fact a plan for a rising in 1797 was considered when Lord Edward sent messengers to France seeking immediate aid. Wolfe Tone joined the Dutch Fleet at Texel and spent three weeks waiting on favourable winds to cross the North sea. James Plunket and William McCabe went to the North to examine preparations for the rising and Lord Edward was smuggled into to Kilmainham to confer with Neilson and McCracken but the rising was postponed when too many difficulties were encountered. However because the call to arms failed to come , many in the North became disheartened and some of the blame was heaped on Plunket. Plunket who was in command in Roscommon failed to turn up to the Convention in February 1798 and it was mainly due to his absence that the '98 rising was postponed until May. However Plunket remained in the confidence of the Directory and he led the United Irishmen when general Humbert landed at Killala. He later surrendered and was allowed to go to England. James Hope said in relation to Plunket;

*"In looking back on the conduct of such men as Plunket, of which there were many in our Society, I do not rank them with the common herd of traitors, they were men who unthinkingly staked more than was in them, -they were like paper money, current for the time, keeping business afloat, but without any intrinsic value!"*5

Meanwhile much of the Leinster Directory were still looking to the continent for aid and assistance.
Hope continued to operate from Dublin until May of 1798. McCracken was released from Kilmainham in December '97 and returned to Belfast. Neilson was released in February of '98 and he remained in Dublin but Russell was held in prison until 1802. In February Arthur O'Connor and Fr. Michael Quigley were arrested at Margate while travelling on United Irish business to Paris. On the 12th of March the entire Leinster Directory with the exception of Lord Edward, were arrested at Oliver Bond's house in Bridge St. on the foot of information supplied to the Castle by Thomas Reynolds a member of the Directory. Leinster House was searched and documents belonging to Lord Edward were confiscated. Lord Edward was forced to go on the run. A decision was made to launch the rising at the earliest possible

moment. Henry Joy McCracken brought the orders to the North that the rising would commence everywhere on May 23rd. James Hope was sent back to Belfast to act as aid-de-camp to Robert Simms who was the Adjutant General for Antrim. On the 19th of May, four days before the rising, Lord Edward was captured in a house in Thomas St. and on the 23rd Samuel Neilson was also captured while trying rescue the Leaders in Newgate prison.

In view of what had happened in Leinster the Officers in the North began to get cold feet. When he saw no action being taken James Hope asked Robert Simms what action he proposed to take. Simms ordered Hope to go to Dunboyne to see if the Rebel forces had assembled there. Along the way Hope met McCracken and explained his mission. McCracken suspected that Simms had no intention of carrying out the orders. He ordered Hope to return to Belfast. When Simms and Hunter were confronted they resigned. Henry Munro and John Coulter were appointed as replacements but when neither could be contacted the position fell to McCracken. Hope then became aid-de-camp to McCracken. Hope was sent to Belfast where he retrieved muskets, musket balls and gunpowder which had been hidden in a book- shop frequented by the United Irishmen. He also retrieved a large green flag, possession of which would have cost him his life.

Hope was despatched with letters and instructions for various officers in the United army. He carried a letter to George Sinclair an appointed officer but he resigned. He relayed another letter through a fellow Unitedman for a senior officer (Rev Steele Dickson) but the United man's wife tore the letter up. Steele Dickson was arrested later on his way to the rendezvous.

This left McCracken Commander-in-Chief of the United Army of Ulster. It was June 4th and McCracken had three days to make his plans.

James hope played an important part in the Battle of Antrim (a fuller account of which will be given in later chapters.) He led the "Spartan Band" which held the line of retreat. He was among the last of McCracken's comrades on the run in the Slemish mountains. He remained in the North until November hiding in various places around the province. He returned to Dublin in 1799 where he joined his family. He worked on a bleach mill in Co. Meath for some months before making a hasty departure narrowly avoiding capture. He worked for Lawrence Tighe in Bluebell Co. Dublin, in whose house Major Swan died after being mortally wounded in the struggle with Lord Edward. Later Hope opened a Draper's shop at No. 8 the Coombe with financial assistance given to him by Charles Teeling.

In 1802 Hope assisted Samuel Neilson, recently released from Fort George, but banished to exile, to travel to Belfast and back to Dublin safely. Neilson was in Ireland at the risk of his life. Hope's greatest gift was his ability to move about the country and remain undetected. In 1803 he was working in his shop in the Coombe when he was approached by James McGucken, a solicitor from Belfast. Thomas Russell had sent a message to a person in Belfast. This person, who was a former friend of Hope's, gave the message to McGucken who then came to Dublin to see Hope and get information about Russell. Hope refused to answer any questions but produced two loaded pistols from underneath the counter. McGucken then said that it was all a joke and suggested that they have a drink and forget it. Hope agreed and sent out for some porter. When McGucken left, Hope paid his rent, packed his bags and vacated the premises. McGucken came back the next day with a party of yeomen but once again Hope had evaded capture. This was the same James McGucken that HenryJoy McCracken had paid to carry out legal work on behalf of Catholics seven years earlier.

Hope then moved to Rathfarnham where he assisted Robert Emmet and Thomas Russell in their preparations for another rising. Hope made two journeys to the North to gather information for Robert Emmet. He brought back word that the North would rise if the Capital was captured. When the rising was declared Hope returned to the North with Russell but their efforts to spark a rising ended in total failure. Hope claimed that he kept Russell perfectly safe until Russell determined to return to Dublin against his advice.

Hope had to flee again and he went live in Drogheda where he worked until 1804. He visited his wife in Dublin occasionally but was never able to stay as he was not safe. He later lived in Westmeath for a while until word came that his wife was ill. He again returned to Dublin where he got work making corduroy. Hope went about armed until 1806 determined never to be taken alive. He went to some lengths to avoid contact with people of a higher class as he considered them totally untrustworthy. When the political climate cooled he returned to Belfast where he worked for John McCracken whom he said treated him badly. However Mary Ann McCracken remained his close friend and benefactor for the remainder of his life. He worked for nine years for an Englishman named William Tucker who treated him with the much fairness and respect.

James Hope was of the greatest assistance to Dr Madden when he was compiling his "Lives of the United Irishmen." and "Antrim and Down '98". Throughout his life James Hope worked hard, took pride in his work and was ready to learn. He cared for his fellow man and was prepared to make sacrifices for the common good. He took pride in his deep distaste for hypocrisy.

His wife Rose died in 1831 and he missed her greatly during the remainder of his life. He lived on in miserable circumstances until 1847 although he remained in contact with Mary Ann McCracken who helped him from time to time. When he died Israel Milkeen, Dr Madden and Mary Ann McCracken had the following memorial erected above his grave;

erected
to the memory of
JAMES HOPE
who was born in 1764 and died in 1847
one of nature's noblest works

AN HONEST MAN

steadfast in faith and always hopeful
of divine protection.
in the best era of his country's history
a soldier in her cause
and at the worst of times still faithful to it
ever true to himself and to those
who trusted in him, he remained to the last
unchanged and unchangeable
*in his fidelity.*6

Samuel Neilson

Samuel Neilson

Samuel Neilson 1761-1803

THE FOUNDER OF THE UNITED IRISHMEN

Samuel Neilson was born in September 1761 in County Down. He received some schooling but was mostly educated by his father. He first worked as a woollen draper for his brother in Belfast. He married into the family of William Bryson, a wealthy merchant and shortly after set-up his own woollen business under the title The Irish Woollen Warehouse. By 1792 his fortune was estimated to be £8000. Neilson was a member of the Northern Whig Club and in 1790 he joined the Volunteers.

The Whigs were liberals who were mainly interested in promoting free trade, that is, they were opposed the restrictions and tariffs that favoured the English over their own native manufacture. One of Neilson's closest friends at this time was Robert Stewart who was also a Northern Whig. However as the Volunteers were sinking into decline and as the Whig Clubs were often seen as nothing more than eating and drinking clubs, Neilson suggested to his other friends HenryJoy McCracken and Thomas Russell that a new club should be set-up which would *"promote a cordial union of the people of Ireland of all religious persuasions"*. Neilson also wanted to seek wider support for parliamentary reform, a policy of the Northern Whig Clubs. By 1791 Neilson had set-up a committee of the leading men of Belfast including William Sinclair, Samuel McTier, Thomas McCabe and Robert and William Simms. Thomas Russell and Theobald Wolfe Tone also became members.

A public meeting was held in Belfast in December 1792 at which Neilson put forward his proposal for a new Society. As a result of this meeting a convention was held in Dungannon early in 1793. After much discussion this convention declared its aims as "Complete Parliamentary Reform and the Immediate Emancipation of Catholics." Around this time Wolfe Tone was promoting the interests of Catholics in Dublin. Tone had been appointed Law Agent to the Catholic Committee and had begun making plans for a great Catholic Convention. He brought the

Catholic Leaders including John Keogh and William Byrne to Belfast where they were warmly received. The promotion of religious liberty was the one great idea conceived by Neilson and from the beginning of his political career until the end he favoured the immediate emancipation of Catholics. It was Thomas Russell who introduced Wolfe Tone's views to Neilson and from Neilson, Tone became interested in the United Irishmen.

Neilson set about organising the Society of the United Irishmen all over the North. His first difficulty was to end the faction fighting between Peep-O-Day Boys and the Catholic Defenders. In July, in the company of Wolfe Tone he went to Rathfryland to restore peace in a row which had broken out between Catholics and Presbyterians. Later in August Neilson and Tone met with Lord Downshire in an effort to have the excesses of the Peep-O-Day Boys curtailed. In September with Charles Teeling, Neilson went to Armagh to intervene between Defenders and Peep-O-Day Boys. Some of these disturbances amounted to a minor civil war and affected the whole community. On another occasion Neilson went with Tone to Portadown to ease troubles between Catholic and Presbyterians. Around this time Neilson had the idea of setting up a Newspaper which would promote unity among the people. Neilson organised a partnership company to launch the newspaper which was called the " Northern Star." There were twelve shareholders and it cost £2000 to launch the paper, but Neilson owned a quarter of the shares and put up £500. Among the shareholders were Robert and William Simms. The first issue appeared on 4th January 1792 and cost two pence. The paper had a regular circulation of 4000 copies throughout its life.

In his first editorial entitled " To The People " Neilson says " *Among the measures essential to the prosperity of Ireland are parliamentary reform, founded on a real representation of the people. To this great object the efforts of the Northern Star will be continued to be extended, until the venal borough trade shall terminate, until corruption shall no longer be publicly avowed and until the common house of parliament shall become the real organ of the public will, then and only then shall the Northern Star in this great business cease. "*[1]

The Northern Star continued in business from 1792 until 1797 when it was destroyed by Orange mobs who wrecked the premises and threw the type and printing equipment out onto the streets of Belfast. It should be noted that the Northern Star was a proper newspaper and not simply a propaganda sheet. Normally consisting of four pages it was published twice a week and was sustained by advertising. Most of its front page was given over to advertisements for rum and seed potatoes. Among the news items reported on; were America, Poland, the black slave trade and the happenings in France. It published a translation of the new French Constitution. Nearly every issue published poetry and it gave a faithful record of the doings in the Irish House of Lords and The Irish House of Commons. It carried numerous letters on various topics and published notices re missing apprentices, who commonly ran away from their employers.

From 1792 until 1797 the Northern Star played an important part in motivating the members of the United Irish Society. But Neilson's friends of former years were now moving in different circles.

The Dublin Whig Club was very much in favour of parliamentary reform in 1791. The Belfast Whig Club was set-up on similar principles and it's most ardent supporters were the Stewarts, not least Robert Stewart. Robert Stewart went forward for election to Parliament 1790 sponsored Samuel Neilson who acted as his election agent. Stewart was contesting the seat against the son of Lord Downshire, on a platform of Parliamentary Reform. But when Stewart won the seat, he proceeded to use his new found power and influence to promote his own personal interests and quickly abandoned his former liberal principles.

Shocked and surprised though Neilson was, this was not the end of their relationship.

From the 1792 until 1796 Samuel Neilson was the driving force behind the United Irishmen. He made most of his converts in the North meeting regularly with Russell, McCracken and Wolfe Tone, but he also took an active part in organising the South. While Russell, McCracken, Hope and Teeling made converts among the poor and the working class, Neilson, Tone and the Simms brothers mixed with the higher echelons of society. While mixing with the ruling class was later scorned at by Hope, it is extremely doubtful if the Society could ever have attained it's aims without the support of people like Bond, Butler, Tandy, Rowan, the Emmets and Lord Edward. The success and growth of the Society in Belfast was never really equalled in Dublin. James hope was probably most successful in organising the ordinary people in the Liberties but the comings and goings and doings of the more noble members were all too open to view and indeed were only a stone's throw from Dublin Castle. Moreover Dublin was awash with spies.

Wolfe Tone's involvement with both the United Irishmen and The Catholic Committee brought him a double dose of odium from the government. He was caught in a trap and was obliged to make a deal with the Government to leave the country in exchange for a withdrawal of prosecution. Before leaving he met with Neilson and the other leading figures in Belfast where they spent a month discussing the country's future and considering the best ways of promoting the unity to which they all aspired. Tone then left for America in July of 1795 having given an assurance to his friends that he would seek French aid at the earliest possible opportunity.

Meanwhile Neilson's erstwhile friend Robert Stewart had befriended Mr. Pitt, the British Prime Minister. It was Mr. Pitt's ambition to effect a union between the parliaments of Britain and Ireland. It was believed by many on the other side of the sea that good relations between all in Ireland could only be achieved by such a union. It would, for example, take important decisions about the country out of the hands of the small ruling elite in Ireland who ruled in their own personal interests. It was known that many Catholics were more in sympathy with the King and the British Parliament than with College Green. Robert Stewart

MP who occasionally held a seat in Westminster decided to support Pitt in his drive for Legislative Union. Lately conferred with the title of Lord Castlereagh he had military experience and led his own militia.

In 1796 having obtained information about the United Irishmen and knowing full well the views of his erstwhile friends, Lord Castlereagh set out to capture the leaders. By 1796 the United Irishmen had four Directories, one for each province. The first Directory formed was the Ulster Directory comprised of Neilson, Robert and William Simms and Dr. White. In September of '96 Castlereagh went north with warrants for the arrest of Russell and Neilson and some of the other leaders. Castlereagh was supported by a large body of cavalry and by Lord Downshire and Lord Westmeath. They entered Belfast and commenced a widespread search. Neither Russell or Neilson were in hiding and they very soon offered themselves up for arrest. The following day they were brought to Newgate prison in Dublin where they were charged with treason. Neilson took the matter rather lightly but Russell was more disturbed. They were forbidden to have pen or paper and were held in solitary confinement. However after a while the prison regime was relaxed. Neilson was later moved to Kilmainham where he joined HenryJoy McCracken who was arrested in October. They were both held throughout 1797 and Neilson was not released until February of 1798. Meanwhile outside the Leinster Directory continued to make plans. Wolfe Tone who had travelled to America and then to France arrived at Bantry Bay in December 1796. The Sheares brothers and Lord Edward who had spent time in France, were fully convinced that only armed revolution would deliver the reforms that the United Irishmen desired. When Neilson was released in February he immediately became a close confidant of Lord Edward who had by that time been appointed Commander-in-Chief of the United Irish Army. A national of convention of United Irish delegates was held at the end of February. It was decided to postpone plans for a rising because the Connaught Delegates were not represented. Within days, the news of the arrest of Arthur O'Connor and Fr. Quigley was superseded by the news of the arrest of the Leinster Directory in Oliver Bond's House. One of Dublin's many spies, Thomas Reynolds a brother-in-law of Wolfe

Tone, and a member of the Directory gave information to Dublin Castle. Lord Edward was forced to go on the run with a price of £1000 on his head. He spent two months hiding in various houses mostly in Dublin's Liberties. Neilson was Lord Edward's prime deputy during this time carrying his messages and meeting delegates, mostly from the North. Neilson visited Lord Edward numerous times in his places of concealment in Cornmarket and in Thomas Street. Neilson and Lord Edward made several night excursions out to view the city and to finalise plans for attacks of various sites within the Capital. One of Neilson's plans was to storm Kilmainham Jail and release the members of the Leinster Directory. Little else is known about the details of the final plans as Lord Edward had to improvise after his documents were seized by the authorities when they raided Leinster House. It was said of Neilson at this time that " *he was riding morning and night to prepare for the rising.* " After the arrest of the Leinster Directory it was decided proceed with rising with or without French assistance at the earliest possible opportunity. May the 23rd was the date appointed for the action to begin and word was sent to the provinces. As final arrangements were being made Neilson had dinner with Lord Edward on the evening of 19th of May in Murphy's of Thomas St. When Neilson left, Lord Edward who was suffering from a cold retired to bed after drinking some whey prepared for him by Murphy. Within an hour the house was raided and Lord Edward was mortally wounded in his efforts to escape. On the 21st of May the Sheares brothers were also arrested as they made their way through the streets of Dublin. On the 23rd the rising commenced with an attack on the Royal Barracks at Naas. The mail coaches were also burned as part of the general signal for the start of hostilities.

Neilson was still free but on his own in Dublin. On the 22nd of May a proclamation was issued offering £300 for the arrest of : Samuel Neilson of Belfast, John Chambers printer, John McCormick feather merchant, William Lawless surgeon and Michael Reynolds of Kildare. With the majority of the leaders in prison the rebels were hamstrung. Neilson decided that the first priority was to free the leaders in Newgate prison. He gathered a group of twenty men with a view to scaling the walls of Newgate but he was arrested while measuring the walls to ascertain the necessary height for the ladders needed. Neilson was recognised by the prison governor Greg who saw him standing outside the prison and ordered him to be arrested. He was set upon by about twelve and was so badly beaten he had bruises over the whole of his body and "was only saved from being killed because his attackers were so many."

Over the following days the rising broke out but all the leading figures, with the exception of HenryJoy McCracken were absent. Most of the other Northern leaders refused to fight, or gave information to the enemy. The rebels had some successes in Kildare, Wicklow and most notably Wexford but many thousands were killed and all the towns captured were quickly lost again. Tone, Tandy and Humbert eventually landed with French help but their missions were also were doomed to failure. On the 26th of June, Samuel Neilson, John and Henry Sheares, John McCann, William Byrne and Oliver Bond were all charged with High Treason. Neilson refused to plead and said he could not afford council as all his property had been stolen by the Government. As a result Neilson was not tried with the others. All the other prisoners were tried, convicted and executed with the exception of Bond who later died of a heart attack while still in prison.

On the 12th of July the Sheares brothers were convicted and executed on the 14th. On the 17th July John McCann was tried and convicted. On this day also HenryJoy McCracken was executed in Belfast. McCann was executed on the 19th. Byrne was executed on the 28th and Oliver Bond was convicted but reprieved. Neilson then entered negotiations with the Government and started a dialogue between the prisoners and the Government about the possibility of a pact or treaty. Neilson explained his proposal to the prisoners as being mainly concerned to save the lives of Byrne and Bond who were still alive when negotiations started. Russell was appalled at the idea of signing any pact with the Government but he agreed to sign it when forced to consider that lives of Byrne and Bond were in his hands. The Pact, otherwise known as the Kilmainham Treaty was drawn up by Neilson and was signed by Arthur O'Connor on behalf of the prisoners in the Bridewell, by Neilson on behalf of the prisoners in Newgate and by Emmet and McNevin on behalf of the prisoners in Kilmainham. The document was signed in the presence of Mr. Secretary Cooke and Lord Castlereagh.

Kilmainham Treaty 29th July 1798

" That the undersigned State Prisoners in the three prisons Newgate, Kilmainham and Bridewell engage to give every information in their power of the whole of the internal transactions of the United Irishmen; that each of them shall give detailed information of everything that has passed between the United Irishmen and foreign states; but that the prisoners are not by naming or describing, to implicate any person whatever, and that they are ready to emigrate to such country as shall be agreed between them and the Government, and not to pass into any enemy's country: if on so doing they are to be free from prosecution and also Mr. Bond be permitted to take the benefit of this proposal. The state prisoners also hope that it may be extended to such prisoners in custody or not in custody as may choose to benefit by it."2

This agreement was signed by all the prisoners on the 29th of July 1798 and it required the signatories to give interviews in which they would tell what they knew about the United Irishmen without giving names. Neilson was examined on the 9th of August in front of Lords Kilwarden, Dillon and Castlereagh. Neilson gave a detailed account of his involvement from 1791 up until his recapture on the 23rd of May '98. During the interview and in answer to questions, he gave his opinions on whether the French would invade, the strength of the United Irish forces at various locations around the country and the best method of quieting the country in the wake of the revolution. He was asked questions in relation to Lord Edward and Mr. Henry Grattan. In answering these questions he got himself into some difficulties for while Lord Edward was now dead, his family was still living and might be affected. Mr. Grattan was still a prominent political figure in Ireland. Neilson refused to answer further questions about either man despite threats from Lord Dillon. In conclusion Neilson recommended that the Government should seek to rule by public opinion and not by force.

28

It was part of the understanding that the prisoners would be allowed to emigrate to America. The prisoners expected this to happen quickly but it was not until March 1799 that they were deported to Scotland after America refused to accept them. Twenty state prisoners including some from Carrickfergus and Belfast Jails were eventually lodged in Fort George in the north of Scotland. In the meantime General Humbert had landed in Killala in August and in December Wolfe Tone was captured and brought ashore at Lough Swilly. Russell became angry when Wolfe Tone could not be included in the pact.

In August a London newspaper called The Courier published details of an Emigration Bill being processed through House of Commons to facilitate 90 prisoners charged with High treason. The paper published statements to the effect that the prisoners had "acknowledged their crimes", "retracted their opinions" and "implored pardon".

Neilson and Russell together with the other prisoners were appalled at these disclosures. They felt the report mis-stated the facts and they were anxious to have a letter of correction printed. Neilson informed Castlereagh of his intention to have such a letter printed. Castlereagh informed Neilson that if such a letter appeared all the executions would be recommenced. The prisoners agreed not to send the letter. Naturally these developments were not conducive to the success of the missions of Humbert, Tandy and Tone.

Neilson and Russell were held in Newgate until the 19th of March 1799 when they were put on board a ship at six in the morning and taken to Scotland but first putting in to Belfast to collect the other state prisoners. Their conditions at Fort George were far superior to anything they had experienced previously. They had more access to fresh air and their family members were allowed to stay with them at the prison. Neilson was held with the other prisoners at Fort George until 1802 when they were deported to Hamburg. During the remainder of his stay he wrote numerous letters especially to his wife who occasionally stayed in

Dublin at the House of Oliver Bond in Bridge St. In one letter he enclosed the following poem to his daughter.

Should we attain the happiest state
That here can be our share
No fleeting pleasures should elate
No grief beget despair
No injury fierce our anger rise
No honour tempt our pride
No vain desires of empty praise
Should in our soul Abide

No charms of youth or beauty move
The constant settled breast
Who leaves a passage free to love
Admits a wily beast
In virtue's path the wealth of life
True peace of mind is found
The greatest blessing God doth give
*Or can on earth be owned.*3
Samuel Neilson Fort George 8th June 1800

Neilson's son William who was only eight years old, joined him at Fort George and spent 18 months living at the jail. At one stage he became very ill and was nursed by the wives of the other prisoners. Neilson's wife, Nancy was never able to visit him in Scotland. While at Fort George the prisoners set up a school for the various children who lived there or stayed for long visits. The following is a letter from Neilson to his wife in 1802.

"William's education goes on to my entire satisfaction, indeed I can hardly say in what branch he does not excel. I count more upon his increasing rectitude of mind than all the rest. So you can guess how much he tends to alleviate my confinement. His daily course comprises; Figures with Mr. Dowling. History with Mr. Emmet, Latin with Mr. Dowdall, Music with Mr. McCormick Mathematics with Mr. Russell and Grammar and Geography with my self."4

Samuel Neilson Fort George Feb. 14th 1802

Neilson left Fort George on 30th June 1802 and sailed for Hamburg. Russell Emmet, Sweeny, Wilson and McCormick had sailed two days earlier. Also freed at this time were Sweetman, Dowling Hudson, McNevin, O'Connor, Chambers, Cuthbert and Cummings. By the time he arrived in Holland, Neilson was already in bad health. Neilson had lost his entire fortune and was now dependent on his friends to help him make his passage to America. Hamilton Rowan who was already living on the continent was the first to offer him assistance. Neilson's first plan was to make straight for America but having encountered delays he changed his mind and in July he decided to try and return to Ireland to bid farewell to his family and friends. There is no doubt that this plan placed his life at serious risk. Nevertheless Neilson succeeded in getting back to Ireland on board an English vessel which landed at Drogheda. He made his way to Dublin where he stayed at the home of Bernie Coile at Lurgan St. He stayed in Dublin for about a week and met many of his old friends including James Hope. Hope brought Neilson safely and successfully to Belfast, both of them travelling on horseback and Hope always proceeding some distance ahead to avoid surprise or capture. Neilson spent three days in Belfast where he met his family and bid them farewell for the last time. He then returned to Dublin where he remained at Irishtown until he obtained a passage for New York. He left from Ringsend in October where he was seen off by his old friends Hope and Palmer. He arrived in New York in December and in his first letter home he reported that his health had worsened considerably due to the voyage. Neilson lived for a further eight months after his arrival in New York but his health continued to deteriorate throughout. He wrote several letters to his family during this period giving an account of the help and hospitality he received from his new friends in America. He had plans to set up a Newspaper of Irish interest and had promises of finance and assistance but he died before this could come to fruition. He died on the 29th of August 1803 at the age of 44 years. Although a Presbyterian his monument was erected by the Catholic organisation The Ancient Order of Hibernians.

Conclusion

There were many moments in Neilson's life where his actions were ambiguous and left him open to doubts. Why did he persuade the prisoners to sign the pact? Was it an attempt to save his own life or was he genuinely concerned about Byrne and Bond.? There are two answers to this question in his favour. Throughout the period of negotiation he shared a cell with Byrne and shared a bed with Bond. Both Mrs Neilson and Mrs Bond were present in the cell when Byrne was called out to be executed. It would surely appear that living in such close proximity to his comrades Neilson could not have suppressed his emotions simply for his own benefit. Secondly, neither Russell or Hope or indeed any of the other prisoners ever doubted his sincerity. In his final situation, banished to America, deprived of his family, having lost his health and his fortune he was still writing about and thinking about his country. Dr. McNevin said of Neilson, " I felt the strongest conviction, the result of a long and familiar acquaintance that Neilson was utterly incapable of treachery to his friend or to his country." Arthur O'Connor said "the imprudent visits Neilson paid to Lord Edward were the cause of his capture. Certainly Neilson never betrayed him!"

Documents eventually came to light which showed Francis Higgins and Francis Mangan of 20 Usher's Island received pensions for information which led to the capture of Lord Edward. Higgins claimed the bounty the following day! And finally, Miss Moore, in whose house in Thomas St. Lord Edward had stayed in safety for several weeks gave the following statement on her death bed in 1844.

*"I can no longer remain silent. Major Sirr got timely information that we were going to Usher's Island. Now this intention was known only to Mangan and to me. Even Lord Edward did not know our destination until just before starting. If Mangan is innocent then I am the informer."*5

Lord
Edward
Fitzgerald

Lord Edward Fitzgerald

Lord Edward Fitzgerald
1763-1798

Lord Edward Fitzgerald was the son of James Fitzgerald, Earl of Kildare and First Duke of Leinster. His mother was Emily Lennox, daughter of the Duke of Richmond. Lord Edward was born on the 15th of October 1763, his father died when he was 10 years old and he spent the rest of his youth in France with his mother and stepfather, a Mr. Ogilive. In 1779 the family returned to London and Lord Edward joined the army where his uncle the new Duke of Richmond was a colonel. In 1780 he became a lieutenant in the 26th Regiment of Foot and was deployed in the south of Ireland. However he shortly transferred to the 19th Regiment of Foot which was then destined for America. While in America he was commended for gallantry in a battle against the Americans led by Colonel Lee, one of America's most distinguished commanders. Also while in America Lord Edward visited the Bahamas and there he met a black man whom he engaged as his personal servant. Always referred as "Tony" this man remained devoted to Lord Edward for the remaining fifteen years of his life. It is reputed that Tony died of a broken heart within weeks of Lord Edward's death.

Soon after Lord Edward's arrival back from America in 1783 his bother the Duke of Leinster arranged his entry into the House of Parliament representing Athy. From '83 until '86 Lord Edward enjoyed a comfortable lifestyle being received in all the best houses in Ireland. He maintained his own main residence at Frescati near Blackrock until 1794. In 1786 Lord Edward enlisted again at Woolwich so he could improve his military expertise. He travelled with his uncle to Guernsey and Jersey to carry out military inspections and later went on to Gibraltar. Having gained sufficient experience he joined the 54th Regiment of Foot which was then leaving for America. While in America on this occasion Lord Edward encountered the American Indians and was greatly impressed by their culture.

He also visited Canada and was moved by the beauty of that country. He returned to England in 1790 and stayed for some time with his mother in London. While in London Lord Edward had dinner with his uncle the Duke of Richmond and with Mr. Pitt the Prime Minister. Lord Edward regaled them with tales of his travels and Mr. Pitt offered to promote Lord Edward and give him command of an expedition to Cadiz. Lord Edward accepted the offer and the Duke of Richmond informed the King. Lord Edward who had held a seat in Parliament for seven years agreed not to renew his seat when the Parliament expired. However unknown to him, his brother the Duke of Leinster had already put his name forward for the constituency of Kildare. This made him a foot soldier of the opposition, while the Duke of Richmond had assured the King that Lord Edward would support the Government. As a result the commission was withdrawn and some ill-will developed between lord Edward and the Duke of Richmond. Lord Edward continued as MP for Kildare from 1790 until 1797. In 1792 The First National Battalion of the Volunteers announced their intention to Parade in Dublin on an appointed date. The Government issued a proclamation banning the march. While Mr. Grattan supported the Government, Lord Edward spoke out strongly against the ban. Although the Government had little intimation that an internal revolt might occur the ongoing developments in France had made them nervous. In February '93 the Arms and Gunpowder Bill was being processed through the house also with the help of Mr. Grattan. Again Lord Edward condemned the act as an "infringement on the liberty of the subject". Lord Edward also opposed the Insurrection Act saying that the " disturbances in the country are not to be remedied by any coercive measures, such measures will tend to exasperate rather than remove the evil".1

Towards the end of 1792 Lord Edward visited Paris, met with, and spent some time in the company of Thomas Paine . Paine had recently gained fame for his book "The Rights of Man." Lord Edward was somewhat in awe of Paine and wrote of him ;

" I lodge with my friend Paine: we breakfast, dine and sup together. The more I see of his interior, the more I like and respect him."2

Lord Edward's close association with Thomas Paine was observed and reported to London. As a result he was expelled from the Army. However while in Paris, Lord Edward came into contact with another important person. He met and married Lady Pamela in Paris on 21st of December 1792. and they returned to Dublin early in 1793 where she was greeted warmly and became very popular in fashionable society.

The Society of the United Irishmen was never properly organised in Dublin prior to the intervention of the Northern Leaders in 1796. The original society set-up by Tandy and Tone with Butler and Bond as its leaders was a wide open affair and was quickly brought to grief when Butler and Bond were imprisoned and Tone and Tandy were forced to flee. It was latterly the influx of leaders like Sweetman, McCormick, Lewins, Byrne and Arthur O'Connor who put the society on a secretive and military footing in 1796. Around this time also Hope and Metcalfe arrived in Dublin to organise the working class. It was the close intimacy between O'Connor and Lord Edward that led him into his association with the United Irishmen. O'Connor was a fellow MP and a frequent visitor to Lord Edward's Home at Frescati prior to him moving out in 1794. They had often been seen together at the races at the Curragh and Lord Edward was impressed by O'Connor's ability as a writer. However their first overt involvement together in the business of the United Irishmen was their journey to the North in 1796. Lord Edward wanted to see for himself what preparations had been made for a possible rising. O'Connor issued a public address to the voters of County Down while they were in the North on that occasion. Later that year O'Connor and Lord Edward went to the Continent to meet Reinhart, the French Minister with a view to obtaining French aid. However even at this first meeting they spoke to intermediaries who passed the word back to Mr. Pitt that Lord Edward was in Hamburg representing the United Irishmen and seeking French help for a rebellion in Ireland. And this was May '96. At a second meeting that year Lord Edward and O'Connor met General Hoche on the borders of France and a treaty was signed between Ireland and France, the first ever such treaty. Lord Edward's approaches had coincided with, and re-enforced the appeals already being made by Wolfe Tone. In September and October of 1796 most of the Northern leaders were arrested and imprisoned. Lord Edward and the other members of the Leinster Directory continued to make plans and to organise the society and they engaged in a continuous communication with the French.

In December 1796 General Hoche led his attempted invasion of Ireland. This left Wolfe Tone bobbing around in Bantry Bay for two weeks but unable to land because of high winds and because General Hoche was lost in the Atlantic. As a result General Lake embarked on a most ferocious campaign of repression throughout the country but particularly against the people of the North. Much energy was devoted during this period to trying to have the Northern Leaders released. By November of '97, in the wake of the failure of the Bantry expedition and with the population of the North having been terrorised into submission, the Government freed most of the Northern leaders although Neilson and Russell were still held. In February of '98 Neilson was released and quickly rejoined his old comrades. He became Lord Edward's prime deputy and Lord Edward was appointed Commander-in-Chief of the United Irish Army. On the 26th of February A National Convention of United Irish Delegates was held in Dublin to make final arrangements for a rising.

Lord Edward addressed the delegates and spoke in favour of an immediate rising saying that they had overwhelming numbers and the Capital could be taken easily. He was supported by delegates from Derry, Antrim, Down, Carlow, Meath and Wicklow. He was opposed by speakers from Dublin who suggested that success was improbable without French assistance. It was also said that there were no middle ranking officers with sufficient military experience. It was further pointed out that Connaught was not represented at the convention. After some heated discussion it was decided to postpone action until Connaught could be consulted and until further news was received from France.

McCracken complained bitterly about those who placed too much faith in the value of French aid. The Northern leaders were seething with anger at the repression and torture which had been inflicted on their people while they were in prison and they were aware that the will to resist was daily ebbing away.

Barely a fortnight after this fateful decision was made the entire Leinster Directory was arrested in the House of Oliver Bond and committed to Kilmainham Jail. Lord Edward's apartments at Leinster House were raided and despite the best efforts of Lady Pamela, a map of Lord Edward's plans for attacks on the city was confiscated by the Castle authorities. Dublin was placed under martial law, a curfew was imposed and a price of £1000 was offered for the capture of Lord Edward Fitzgerald. About this time Lord Edward's step father, Mr Ogilive came to Dublin and had in interview with Lord Clare. Lord Clare said of Lord Edward " for God's sake, get this young man out of the country: the ports shall be thrown open to you, and no hindrance whatever offered."

Mr. Ogilive tried to persuade Lord Edward to leave but his last word was, "it is now out of the question; I am too deeply pledged to these men to withdraw with honour."3 It was also suggested to Lord Edward by some of the United Irishmen that it would be more beneficial if he stayed in the background. He said " I know my duty, I will not shirk it, I must lead my people."4

Lord Edward then went into hiding in Dublin. He spent the first weeks at a cottage in Harold's Cross near Mount Jerome. Then he went to Kennedy's of Aungier street and after a few days moved to the Home of Mrs Dillon at Portobello. At this time his wife and children were living at Denzile street and he visited them there and saw them and his servant Tony for the last time at this address. Being black Tony could not move about the city without attracting attention. Lord Edward stayed at Mrs Dillon's for three weeks in perfect safety. From there he moved to Murphy's the feather merchant in Thomas street where he remained in safety for a further two weeks. During his stay at this address he was visited by James Plunket chief commander of the Connaught forces of The United Irishmen. From there Lord Edward moved to the home of John McCormick also in Thomas street. Here he was visited by Thomas Reynolds and John Hughes both of whom were paid informers, but neither of whom betrayed his whereabouts to the Government at that time. Lord Edward then moved to the Home of Mr Gannon of Cornmarket where he stayed for a number of days. Early in May he set out in disguise with Neilson for County Kildare to examine the terrain and to decide where best to stage attacks on Crown positions. On their return they were stopped by a Yeoman patrol at Palmerstown and were only allowed to continue when they convinced the patrol that they were a doctor and patient returning his surgery. Subsequent to this Lord Edward moved to the home of James Moore, also in Thomas street. He remained there in safety for some days until a carpenter, working in Dublin Castle overheard Secretary Cooke giving instructions that Moore's premises should be raided for pikes and firearms. The carpenter left the Castle (to obtain a hinge) and ran with the information to Moore's in Thomas street. When Moore got the information he fled to Maynooth leaving his daughter to take care of Lord Edward. Moore's daughter (who was a staunch member of the United Irish Society and a senior confidant of the Executive) went to the Home of Francis Mangan a Catholic Barrister and a former United Irishman and asked him to provide shelter for Lord Edward. Mangan readily agreed and suggested that they enter his home later that evening by the back entrance near the stables, as a large party at the front door might arouse suspicion. Mangan then conveyed this information to Dublin Castle through his legal friend, Francis Higgins a judge in the High Court and the proprietor of the Freeman's Journal. Mr. Cooke informed Major Sirr that Lord Edward and a party would walk towards Usher's Quay that evening at 8.o'clock and that a watch should be placed at Watling Street and at Dirty Lane.

Later that evening Lord Edward, Miss Moore, her mother and his bodyguards McCabe, Gallagher. Palmer and Rattigan walked from Thomas Street down Watling Street. Having been previously warned, Major Sirr was lying in wait having divided his party between Usher's Island and Watling street. When Major Sirr recognised Lord Edward he seized him but Lord Edward had arranged his body guards so that Major Sirr was then surprised by Gallagher and Rattigan who were walking on the far side of the street. Major Sirr was knocked to the ground and stabbed several times, but wearing chain-mail under his clothes he was not injured. In the melee Lord Edward escaped and made his way to Murphy's house where he had stayed previously.

McCabe (Thomas Putnam) was injured in the second clash when the alternative parties met at Usher's Island and although they escaped, he was later captured and identified by his injuries. Lord Edward then planned to move to the home of Mrs Risk in Sandymount. However the following day the streets were saturated with soldiers and no move could be made. In constant fear of being searched Murphy (who was never a United Irishman) persuaded Lord Edward to climb up onto the roof and hide in the valley between the two buildings of his house and his factory. Lord Edward who was suffering from a cold, lay like this for some hours in great discomfort. In the meantime Major Sirr carried out an intensive search of Moore's house. Mangan who had been expecting Lord Edward the previous evening then called at Moore's and asked what had happened. Miss Moore told him about the fight and that Lord Edward *"was now safe at Murphy's. "*5

Later that afternoon a woman arrived at Murphy's with a bundle of clothes for Lord Edward. When Murphy opened the bag he found a magnificent uniform in red and green with a cocked hat and gold braid and gold epaulets. He hid the uniform in his feather warehouse. That evening Samuel Neilson arrived and had dinner with Lord Edward and Murphy. After dinner Neilson left (suddenly according to Murphy) and Murphy made a hot drink of whey and sherry for Lord Edward who drank it and retired to bed.

Within a few minutes Major Sirr with a large party raided the house. The first to enter was Major Swan as Major Sirr was placing guards around the house. When Major Swan entered the bedroom Lord Edward sprang up from the bed like a tiger and produced a dagger with which he stabbed Major Swan several times. Swan drew a pistol from his waistcoat pocket and fired at Lord Edward grazing his right shoulder. Lord Edward continued to fight stabbing Major Swan again and fatally wounding Captain Ryan who was next closest to him. Swan fled down the street bleeding profusely his shirt in tatters. Major Sirr by then had

41

arrived at the top of the stairs. He fired his pistol at Lord Edward wounding him in the arm and forcing him to drop his dagger. Lord Edward was then brought down by weight of numbers and held on the ground and had his hands tied.

With the soldiers surrounding the house Lord Edward's bodyguard was alerted. Rattigan (who was in charge of the watch house at St. Catherine's where the United Irishmen had stored their arms and pikes) ran to the watch house and grabbed all the arms he could carry, shared them out among the local people and urged them to join in the struggle to free Lord Edward. (Major Sirr's men had to pass St. Catherine's on their way back to the Castle.) A large group of people then set upon Major Sirr and his soldiers who included about twelve of the Dunbarton Fencibles, but they were prevented from effecting Lord Edward's escape by the arrival of the Dublin cavalry who arrived from the Castle just in time to save Major Sirr. Lord Edward was then taken to the Castle in a sedan chair but not before he was injured on the back of the neck by a Drummer Boy who struck him while he was lying on the ground. This injury caused him the greatest agony during his remaining days.

Murphy was arrested and spent twenty three weeks in prison. Worse for him, his house was thrown open to looters who robbed him of all his possessions, a loss amounting to over £2000. Rattigan's furniture was dragged out on to the street and set on fire by the soldiers.

Lord Edward was brought from the Castle to Newgate prison where Thomas Russell was able to spent the first night with him. Lord Edward was held in the most comfortable room in the prison. He was attended by two surgeons every day. However after the first night the Government ordered him to be held in solitary confinement. He was not allowed to have any visitors and even his family were prevented from seeing him although everyone knew he was seriously ill. He was under the care of Lieutenant Stone of the Londonderry Regiment who Lord Edward commended for his humanity. Russell believed that Lord Edward died of pneumonia when his cold continuously worsened.

Lord Edward continued to deteriorate over a period of two weeks to a point where he was consumed by fever. Matthew Dowling, one of the State prisoners sent a letter to Lord Henry Fitzgerald informing him that his brother was dying. Lords Clare and Castlereagh gave permission to Lord Henry and Lady Louisa Connolly to visit him on Sunday 3rd June at twelve midnight. Lord Edward died the following day the 4th of June 1798, the day on which the rebels in Wexford captured the town of Gorey.

Lord Edward's body was secretly interred in the basement of St. Wergburgh's Church marked only by scratch marks on the coffin lid.6

In the aftermath of Lord Edward's death, Lord Henry wrote to Lord Camden, the Viceroy, who had refused Lord Henry access to Lord Edward (and had heartlessly rejected the tear-filled pleas of Lady Louisa) accusing him of ill-treating his brother, of driving him mad and of persecuting him to the edge of his grave. Within a fortnight, Lord Camden was sacked as Viceroy and replaced by Lord Cornwallis who sanctioned the pact with prisoners.

Conclusion

It is quite clear from reported arguments between Lord Edward and Dr. McNevin that Lord Edward was always in favour of an early rising. He was anxious for and would readily accept any help he could get from the French. However he was not prepared to wait indefinitely for the French to land and except for the opposition from some of the southern delegates he would surely have agreed to an earlier rising rather than to hide in the Liberties for three months. The failure of Dublin to take any active part in the events of 1798 has often been discussed. It is often thought that in the 1916 rising, Dublin atoned for it's omissions during previous struggles. The finding of Lord Edward's map in a glass case in Leinster House during a search in early March, left the organisation in Dublin and its plan of attack in grave danger. The capture of Dublin was Lord Edward's prime responsibility and he had set this as the catalyst that would spark the revolution in the country as a whole. Moreover, Lord Edward was perceived by all the United Irish delegates as the only one with sufficient military experience to carry the rising to success. It is quite possible that the United Irishmen in Dublin were paralysed by the absence of their leaders, the absence of a plan or by the knowledge that the plan was already in the hands of the Government who had trebled the guard on all important positions. Lord Edward claimed to have a quarter of a million men signed up for the rising. He knew that they were indisciplined. He said that this did not matter; that sheer weight of numbers would win the day. The English had no army of any consequence relying on locally recruited militia to maintain their rule. Most of England's forces were on the high seas fighting the French and protecting their commercial shipping. The English interest in Ireland was being maintained by moving yeomen and militia to fight in counties where they would not be recognised. The English were vulnerable, but only so long as the morale of the United Irishmen could be maintained. The English broke the morale of the United Irishmen by spending money! A poor man cannot play poker with a millionaire. They bought the press, they bought the judiciary and they bought their informers. It was estimated by Charles Vane, a brother of Lord Castlereagh, that the Government spent £3000,000 buying support for its policies in Ireland in 1798 alone. Lord Edward, by his own hand-written account had £1,485.4s9d.

end.

Theobald Wolfe Tone

Theobald Wolfe Tone

Theobald Wolfe Tone
1763-1798

Theobald Wolfe Tone was the father of Irish republicanism. He was the first major figure from the Protestant class to openly espouse complete emancipation for Catholics. He was the driving force behind the Catholic convention of 1792 and he persuaded the French Government on three separate occasions to commit substantial resources, in men and materials, in an effort to wrest Ireland form British control.

Wolfe Tone was highly esteemed by Henry Joy McCracken, Samuel Neilson and Thomas Russell. He was honoured by Bonaparte and Carnot and widely respected even by the British. His life was complicated, his character complex and the age in which he lived was one of confusion and turmoil.

Wolfe Tone was born on the 20th of June 1763 at Stafford Street Dublin. He was the eldest of five children having three brothers and one sister. His second youngest brother Matthew joined the French army and landed with General Humbert at Kilalla in 1798. Wolfe Tone's father, Peter Tone was a coach builder who also owned property in Dublin , Drogheda and Kildare. Their home at Stafford Street was comfortable and Wolfe Tone was used to having servants help him deal with the less agreeable aspects of life. He obtained his early education at a school in Stafford street but was always a reluctant student. When Wolfe Tone was fifteen years old his father's coach building business fell into bankruptcy and Wolfe Tone was left in Dublin to continue his schooling while his family returned to Bodenstown. His father had a cottage and a small piece of land there.. Wolfe Tone took advantage of his father's absence and spent most of his time in the Phoenix Park watching military parades. From this early experience Wolfe Tone developed a great ambition to become a soldier. Wolfe Tone's father however, was determined that his son should become a lawyer and he ordered his son to return to his studies. Eventually Wolfe Tone entered Trinity College in February 1781 but being as reluctant as ever it took him five years to graduate. While at Trinity, Wolfe Tone lived at the home of Richard Martin MP. Otherwise known as Humanity Dick, Martin was a wealthy landowner who had installed a private theatre in his house in Kildare Street to amuse his wife, who was very beautiful, and a talented amateur actress. Wolfe Tone fell deeply in love with Mrs Martin and although they never engaged in an affair, Wolfe Tone and the MP quarrelled and Wolfe Tone was forced to seek new lodgings. Shortly after he had graduated Wolfe Tone met and married Matilda Witherington a fifteen year old girl who lived with her grandfather Richard Fanning in Grafton Street. Tone did not seek the approval of Mr. Fanning but instead married Matilda in a "runaway marriage" and after spending a few Days in Maynooth they returned to Dublin where the "fait accompli" was accepted. Wolfe Tone had by now resigned himself to a career in law. This meant that he was obliged to spend two years at the Middle Temple in London before he could be called to the bar. Leaving his wife and child in the care of the Witheringtons he set out for London with financial assistance from Theobald Wolfe a landowner in Kildare with whom his father had a business relationship and after whom Wolfe Tone was called.

Between 1786 and '88 Wolfe Tone lived in London and indulged himself in much of the decadence that passed for good living in the 1780's. However during this time he made new connections, not least of whom was George Knox who was to be important in his future life. While in London, Tone earned money by writing for various periodicals such as the European Magazine to which he contributed several reviews. Also while in London Wolfe Tone drafted a plan for the colonisation of Hawaiian Islands which he presented to Mr. Pitt in person. When Mr. Pitt failed to act on the plan Tone was disappointed and bitter.

At the end 1788, having fulfilled the requirements, i.e. eating dinner three times in each term in the common hall of the Middle Temple, he was now qualified for a career in law. His wife's grandfather agreed to give him £500 to open a law practice in

Dublin. Wolfe Tone and his family then moved to Clarendon Street and having taken his degree he was called to Bar in May 1789. Wolfe Tone then took the oaths of adjuration and allegiance which were set out in the parliamentary Acts of 1704,1710 and 1766 designed to " prevent the further growth of popery." He first practised law on the Leinster circuit with cases in Wicklow, Kilkenny and Carlow. Being fairly successful he cleared most of his debts by the end of his first circuit.

Wolfe Tone then became interested in writing pamphlets. Several of his legal contemporaries had already done this successfully and profitably. His first published pamphlet was called " A Review of the Conduct of Administration." In this pamphlet he made a vigorous attack on the Government and this greatly pleased the Whig opposition. Tone had signed himself "An Independent Irish Whig" and when the Whigs discovered who had written it they elected him a member of their club. In his second pamphlet which he signed " Hibernicus " Tone questioned whether Ireland was bound to support Britain in the future probable war with Spain. As a result of this pamphlet Tone fell out of favour with the Whigs who while strongly opposed to the Governments domestic policy, always supported London's foreign policy. In July of 1790, after the general election, the Dublin parliament voted £200,000 to prepare Ireland against possible invasion.

Wolfe Tone was by now spending more and more time in the gallery of the House of Commons and there he met Thomas Russell, a soldier recently retired from service in India. Russell and Tone struck up an immediate friendship and over the following weeks they spent much time in discussing politics, war and Ireland's relationship to Great Britain. In the meantime Matilda's grandfather died, leaving her nothing in his will and she was now in bad health. Wolfe Tone rented a cottage in Irishtown where his wife could benefit from the sea air. Wolfe Tone and Thomas Russell spent a pleasant summer by the sea discussing politics and considering the events in France, i.e. the French revolution which had occurred the previous year. All of Europe was enthralled by this event which had only ever been equalled by the rise of Oliver Cromwell one hundred and fifty years earlier. At length Thomas Russell was promoted and deployed to take up a commission with a Regiment in Belfast. Before leaving, Tone gave Russell introductions to the Knox family with whose son Tone had studied in London. Russell quickly established himself in Belfast becoming very popular with the many radicals in the city whose constant topic of conversation was the French revolution . Another topic of conversation in Belfast at that time was the repression of the Catholic population who were deprived of a large range of civil rights. Northern Dissenters, mostly Presbyterians also had their own grievances and were anxious for a reform of the Dublin Parliament which they considered to be failing to protect them from unfair trade tariffs which operated in favour of England. The publication of Thomas Paine's treatise, "The Rights of Man " was also received with great enthusiasm by the people of Belfast at this time.

A committee was set-up to arrange a celebration of the storming of the Bastille, to be held in Belfast on the 14th of July 1792. Wolfe Tone himself had already taken a great interest in these developments and had written a pamphlet under the Title " An argument on behalf of Catholics " in August 1791. This was published by Edward Byrne, a Dublin printer and sold for a shilling a copy. In this clever pamphlet Wolfe Tone managed to evoke the sympathy of the Northern Dissenters for the Catholic cause by pointing up the similarities between the grievances of both and by dwelling on the new-found ideas contained in documents such as the " Rights of Man." This pamphlet was an immediate success and the first print run of 6000 copies was quickly sold. A second printing of 10,000 copies was just as quickly distributed. Wolfe Tone had already visited his friend Russell in Belfast in 1791 where he was introduced to Samuel Neilson, HenryJoy McCracken and Robert Simms. After the publication of his third pamphlet Wolfe Tone was invited by his new friends to draft an address to The People of Ireland to be presented at the Bastille Day celebration in Belfast on the 14th of July. However, Tone was warned by Neilson that not all the radicals in Belfast were fully in favour of Catholic emancipation. Tone then carefully crafted an address which set out the grounds for a fundamental reform of the Irish Parliamentary system, encompassing tolerance for "every religious persuasion " and at the same time was careful not to over-emphasise the republican nature of his proposals.

His address was enthusiastically embraced, Wolfe Tone was the toast of Belfast and on his return to Dublin he was appointed assistant secretary to the Catholic Committee.

The Catholic Committee had recently been taken over by more radical Catholics such as John Keogh, William McNevin and Edward Lewins. All these were from the merchant middle class and they had replaced the former leaders, mostly wealthy landowners, who were cautious and conservative and slow to press for the rights of ordinary Catholics. Keogh in particular was an able leader, having started out in poor circumstances he had built himself a large fortune and at fifty years of age, he was devoting his time to promoting the rights of his fellow Catholics. Already some of the harsher measures of the penal laws had been repealed with the Catholic Relief Acts passed in 1778 and 1782, but Catholics still could not vote, sit in parliament take commissions in the army or engage in the legal professions. These official disbarments engendered a culture whereby Catholics were treated as second class citizens in all other aspects of life also. Wolfe Tone was officially appointed Law Agent to the Catholic Committee on the 24th of July 1792 on a contract and a salary of £200. He immediately set about organising the National Convention which was to be held in December of the same year. Many of the more conservative elements of the Catholic leadership were reluctant to meet in a National Convention and Wolfe Tone engaged in a campaign to ensure a maximum attendance. Any split in the ranks of the Catholics would play into the hands of those who were opposed to the reforms being sought. Wolfe Tone's campaign was successful and on the 3rd of December 1792 two hundred and thirty five delegates assembled in the Tailor's Hall in Dublin, the first such gathering of Catholic representatives for over a hundred years. Among those attending were Dr. Troy Archbishop of Dublin and Dr. Moylan Bishop of Cork.

The Convention passed two resolutions;

" That the Catholics peers, prelates and delegates chosen by the people are the only power competent to speak on behalf of the Catholics of Ireland. "

and

*" That a petition be presented to the King stating our grievances and praying for relief. "*1

Five delegates were appointed including Edward Byrne and John Keogh to go to London, to see the King and to present the petition. Wolfe Tone was to accompany them as secretary and law agent.

The delegates travelled to London via Belfast where Wolfe Tone introduced them to his friends and where they received a very warm reception form the Presbyterians in that city. When the delegates arrived in London, early in 1793 they were received courteously by the King who accepted their petition and as a result they returned to Dublin satisfied in their mission. On the 10th of January, when the parliament re-opened the King's speech contained the following sentence "His Majesty trusts that the situation of His Majesty's Catholic subjects will engage your serious attention and in the consideration of this matter, relies on the wisdom and liberality of His parliament."

By April a Bill had been passed giving Catholics with property the right to vote, they were also permitted to enter Trinity, to engage in the Legal profession and to take-up various civil and military positions. They were still excluded from parliament and Wolfe Tone was annoyed by this omission. Nevertheless these changes were the most important positive benefits achieved by the Catholic Committee and were largely due to Wolfe Tone's organising zeal.

However a totally different event occurred in the Spring of 1793. War broke between England and France. As a result, the Government brought in a number of security measures. The

Arms and Gunpowder Act. and the Insurrection Act. were just two of the measures which caused a major controversy in the country that year. Wolfe Tone's radical friends in Belfast , Neilson, Russell and Simms had established the Society of the United Irishmen as early as October 1791. This "club" was intended to promote greater understanding between Irishmen of all religious creeds and to campaign for civil rights for Catholics and dissenters alike. Wolfe Tone was loosely associated with the Society and had drafted a declaration for them in 1792. An off-shoot of the Society was also set-up in Dublin in 1792 with Simon Butler as chairman and Oliver Bond as secretary. James Tandy, who had been a leading figure in the Irish Volunteers and who had led their mass rally in Dublin in 1792, was also a leading member. However the Dublin Society of the United Irishmen encountered troubles from very the outset of its existence. While the Northern Society was constantly growing and having beneficial effects throughout the Province, the Dublin Society quickly became embroiled in local politics and personal lawsuits. Although some of the most respected citizens of the city were associated with it, the Society became little more than a talking shop. Wolfe Tone attended some of the meetings but he was always disappointed with the progress of the Society in Dublin. He was far more impressed with the people of Belfast who were equally quick to show their respect for him. With the new Catholic reforms in place Wolfe Tone began to take an even greater interest in the campaign for parliamentary reform.

The Dublin Government, having placated the Catholics to a degree, now felt in a stronger position to resist the demands of the Dissenters. The main demands of the Presbyterian merchant and manufacturing class of Belfast was for an equal and fair representation in Parliament, i.e. universal suffrage. They also wanted the removal of all the trade tariffs which favoured English over native produce. The Society of the United Irishmen had incorporated these demands into their platform alongside the demand for Catholic emancipation. The Dublin Government sought to break Irish Unity by placating the Catholics to a certain extent, and at the same time repressing the dissenters. The Gunpowder Bill and the Insurrection Act. were aimed specifically at them. The Irish Volunteers, mainly a Protestant and Presbyterian force was disbanded because of their vigorous support for parliamentary reform. With these new measures in place, the Government instituted arms searches throughout the Province of Ulster, where the Presbyterians had previously been allowed to keep their own arms. The Government sent extra troops to Belfast, who deliberately provoked riots and then rapidly disarmed the long-standing Volunteers.

Meanwhile in Dublin, the Government set up a select Committee of the House of Lords to examine witnesses and to enquire into possible subversion.. Butler and Bond published a paper condemning the Government's action and saying the committee was unconstitutional. They were speedily arrested and held in prison without trial for six months and fined £500 each. It also emerged that a letter, written by Wolfe Tone to Thomas Russell, had fallen into the hands of the Government. Lord Fitzgibbon in particular, wanted to find a way of ending the career of Theobald Wolfe Tone. Russell was summoned before the committee but he refused to answer any questions implicating Tone. The Government failed to obtain credible evidence against Wolfe Tone but nevertheless, Lord Fitzgibbon read out his private letter in the House of Lords and warned the House against the dangers of the United Irishmen.

Throughout 1793 the Government gathered information and bribed witnesses in an effort to blacken the name of the United Irishmen. Hamilton Rowan was convicted of having traitorous dealings with the French and sentenced to two years in prison on the basis of perjured evidence given by paid witnesses. Some of the jury were also paid for their verdict on this occasion. Early in 1794 the Government raided the rooms of the Society in Dublin and seized their papers and publications. From this point on the Society was compelled to operate underground and in secret. Also, because of the wide spread repression the attitude and aims of the society began to alter. Members felt that the Government could not be trusted to act fairly or within the law. More radical aims and more radical methods began to take hold.

About this time Wolfe Tone was introduced to William Jackson by Edward Lewins who was fast becoming an extremist. It turned out that Jackson, who to all appearances was an English man, was in fact an Irish man and a paid agent of the French. Both Jackson and Tone visited Hamilton Rowan who was at that time held in Newgate Prison. There all three discussed the likelihood of a rising in Ireland and whether the Irish would welcome French assistance. Wolfe Tone agreed to draft up a memorandum in which he described the people of Ireland as " hating the very name of England arising from a tyranny of nearly seven hundred years." He also said that " they would probably throw off the yoke, if they saw any force in the country to whom they could resort for defence." He then pointed out that the "Ulster Dissenters were the most likely to lead the revolt."2 Tone would not allow this memorandum to be conveyed to Paris in his own handwriting but he allowed Hamilton Rowan to make several copies which Jackson then posted to the French Ministry in Hamburg. These Letters were intercepted by the British and Jackson was arrested in April 1794. Rowan realising the grave danger he was now in, bribed his way out of Newgate and fled to America.

Wolfe Tone approached the Government through some of his influential friends and agreed to give a full account of his own involvement in return for a promise of immunity. George Knox and Marcus Beresford negotiated on Tone's behalf. Tone agreed to emigrate to America but refused to give evidence against Jackson. On the pretext of these disclosures the government quickly moved to suppress the United Irish Societies. The Government were secretly pleased developments, as they were more justified in the eyes of London in adopting their harsh measures. The trial of Jackson was delayed for nearly a year during which time Wolfe Tone was left in a state of limbo. By then there was much sympathy for Jackson and most people thought he would be acquitted. In fact he was found guilty of Treason and would have hanged only he committed suicide, taking poison while standing in the dock! Wolfe Tone was embarrassed by Jackson's trial particularly as his name was mentioned numerous times during the court proceedings. Tone published an account of his agreement with the Government and claimed that he had acted with honour throughout.

Wolfe one was now forced to leave Ireland. He first went to Rathfarnham with Thomas Russell to visit Thomas Emmet. While there they discussed the future of the United Irish Society. Tone explained his plan to use America as a stepping stone to France where he would seek French aid for a rising and they would strike for the complete freedom of Ireland. Meanwhile the Catholic Committee paid Wolfe Tone the outstanding money which they owed him, approximately £1500. He left Dublin on the 20th of May 1795 and made his first stop at Belfast. There he was warmly received, and once again was treated like Royalty for nearly four weeks. Most famously he attended parties in the homes of HenryJoy McCracken and John Templeton and attended a very special picnic held on Cave Hill outside Belfast. At this picnic all the leading figures of the United Irish Society made a solemn compact " never to desist in our efforts until we have subverted the authority of England over our country and asserted her independence." On the 15th of June 1795 Wolfe Tone and his family set off for America on board the "Cincinnatus". After an uncomfortable journey on board this small ship with 300 other passengers they landed at Wilmington on the 1st of August. While in America Tone met up with many other exiled United Irishmen and the state of things back home and the ongoing repression was a constant topic of conversation among them. Wolfe Tone considered the possibility of settling down with his family in America but he found the manners and customs of the people to be far too crude and ignorant. Having received letters of appeal from Russell, Neilson and Keogh he decided to proceed with his original plan and carry on to Paris. Robert Simms sent him Exchange Bills to the values of £200 and having made arrangements for his family to remain in America he booked a passage to France which left from New York on the 1st of January 1796. After a trouble free journey he landed at Le Harve on the 1st of February. The first thing Wolfe Tone noticed when he arrived was how cheap wine, food and lodgings were in comparison to America, Britain and Ireland. He was able to stay at the best Hotels for twenty-five pence a night. He also noticed that there was a plentiful supply and a wide variety of food which was contrary to all the propaganda of the British. Wolfe Tone attended the Opera and was highly impressed by the confidence of the ordinary citizens. Although he had letters of introduction from the French Ambassador in America, he encountered severe difficulties in persuading the French that he could speak with authority about the situation in Ireland. The French treated Wolfe Tone with the greatest respect but they were constantly seeking fresh information from Ireland. Wolfe Tone became increasing annoyed because the French misunderstood the position in Ireland. Wolfe Tone met Carnot, Bonaparte, Clare and Hoche and all were impressed by him and expressed their admiration for his courage and his sacrifice. Awarding him a high rank in the French army, the French Government subsidised what was in effect the Irish embassy in Paris. However, it was only after Lord Edward and Arthur O'Connor met with French representatives that they were convinced that there was widespread support for a rising. Edward Lewins, who was Lord Edward's emissary to Paris worked closely with Wolfe Tone from this point on. Napper Tandy who was also in Paris, however was less co-operative and caused confusion by making different demands on the French. Wolfe Tone wanted the French to land at Belfast, Lord Edward wanted them to Land at Drogheda and Wexford and Napper Tandy wanted them to land in Galway. As a result the French decided to land at Bantry Bay in County Cork. It had taken the Irish ten months to convince the French that Ireland was ripe for invasion but it was now December, the worst possible time to launch a fleet of warships. Nonetheless, Wolfe Tone was delighted that his mission to France had been successful and a strong force of forty five ships set sail for Ireland. Measures were taken to fool the British into thinking that the Fleet was bound for Portugal. This tactic may have worked for the armada never encountered any enemy fire throughout the entire voyage. Wolfe Tone was on board the "Indomptable" while the Commander-in-Chief, General Hoche was on board a fast frigate the Fraternité. The fleet sailed south to fool the British, the intention being to change direction when sufficiently far out to sea (and away from the eyes of spies and sentries). However, when changing direction a confusion ensued because of thick fog, and when the fog cleared only thirty-four of the ships were still on course for Bantry Bay. Worst of all, the Fraternité, with the Commander-in-Chief, the money and the invasion plans on board, were no where to be seen, and indeed not seen again until they arrived back at Le Harve on the 14th of January '97. On December 22nd, seventeen ships, including the "Indomptable" were anchored offshore in Bantry Bay. Another seventeen ships were gradually making their way onto the bay. On December the 23rd a heavy gale blew twenty of the ships back out to sea. Over the next four days the French ships entered or left the bay constantly fighting high winds which made them difficult to manoeuvre. The commanders on board the vessels seemed paralysed by the absence of General Hoche. A secret part of each captain's instructions was that in the event of the fleet breaking up they were to head for the mouth of the Shannon and this many of them did on 27th of December. However, while some ships were leaving for the Shannon, others were just arriving for the first time at Bantry Bay. General Hoche arrived at Bantry after most of the other ships had left. A French historian later pointed out that " for fourteen days French ships had been anchored in Bantry Bay between 22nd of December and the 6th of January, and 14000 troops could have landed without any obstacle from the British Navy." Wolfe Tone's ship arrived back in Brest on the 1st of January at which point he was engulfed in frustration and despair.

However Wolfe Tone's family had just arrived from America and he went to visit them in Hamburg, as his wife was too ill to travel any further. Tone and his family visited Amsterdam and they had pleasant time there before they returned to Paris. Meanwhile General Hoche, who had recently defeated the Austrians in a major battle, gave Wolfe Tone an improved commission in the French Army.

In June 1797 Lord Edward sent Edward Lewins to Paris to press the French for immediate aid as the situation in Ireland was desperate. Both he and Wolfe Tone met with General Hoche and persuaded him to send letters to the Directory and the Ministry of the Marine asking for a new expedition to Ireland. They both agreed but the Ministry wanted to send a large expedition while Tone was against this because it would involve too much delay. General Hoche suggested that the Dutch Fleet, of seventeen ships at Texel on the North Sea could be used straight away. Wolfe was delighted with this suggestion and set out for Texel on the 8th of July. The Dutch fleet was in excellent condition and the soldiers were anxious for a fight with the British who had defeated them in a earlier battle. However between July and September both winds and tides operated against the fleet putting to sea. Meanwhile Wolfe Tone was receiving regular news of the ongoing persecutions in Ireland. His friends Neilson, Russell and McCracken were all in prison and General Lake was engaged in a campaign of terror throughout the whole island of Ireland. At the same time a row broke out in Paris between members of the Directory. Carnot fled and General Hoche died of a sudden illness. Wolfe Tone went to Paris to seek a change of plan. The Dutch fleet were ordered to sea and defeated in a battle against the British at Campedown. In desperation Wolfe Tone, Lewins and some other United Irishmen in Paris gave a dinner at Meot's Restaurant in honour of the leading French generals. They also had a meeting with Tallyrand the Minister for Foreign Affairs. They were assured that an expedition to Ireland would be ready by April 1798. In December they were invited to meet Napoleon who seemed to know little about Ireland but agreed with the plans being made by his generals. Wolfe Tone was given the post of Adjutant General in the "Army of England" and he joined the fleet a Rouen at the end of March. On April the 5th Napoleon and General Desaix inspected the western ports and declared that they were not sufficiently prepared for the invasion of England. Within weeks of this decision the English attacked the French ports and Wolfe Tone was engaged in defending the port of Le Harve while the rebellion in Ireland was collapsing. Early in June news came through of the rising in Ireland. Tone and Lewins were shocked to hear of the arrest and death of Lord Edward. The French announced that they were postponing their invasion to a more suitable time. They said that they could not mount a large expedition and would not risk a small one. Tone and Lewins were desperate. In view of the rising they demanded an immediate expedition of " even 5000 men ". Their attitude was "its now or never." In July the French agreed to send three small expeditions under Generals Hardy, Humbert and Kilmaine. Humbert was to leave immediately with 1000 men followed by Hardy with 3000 and finally Kilmaine would follow with 9000. However with the usual delays it was August the 6th by the time Humbert set sail and 23rd of August before he landed at Killala. in Co. Mayo. By this time nearly all the local resistance had been stamped out. Wolfe Tone's brother Matthew and his friend Bartholomew Teeling landed with General Humbert. After their defeat at Ballinamuck they were arrested taken to Dublin, tried and hanged. General Humbert surrendered and was treated as a prisoner of war. It was 16th of September when Wolfe Tone set out for Ireland again with General Hardy aboard the Hoche. Hardy's fleet consisting of nine ships and 3000 men reached the coast of Donegal on the 10th of October 1798. Hardy had taken a detour out into the Atlantic in the hope that they could evade pursuit. But the English knew that they were coming and they also knew that Wolfe Tone was among them. They lay in wait and a great sea battle ensued in which Sir John Warren, the English commander led his men to victory over the French Fleet. Although the Battle took place on the 12th of October it was the 3rd of November before the ships finally reached land due to ferocious storms of the Donegal coast. As General Hardy sailed into Lough Swilly he was amazed that this excellent natural harbour had been overlooked in previous planning. The prisoners were taken ashore at Buncrana and Wolfe Tone was among the first to be placed in irons. General Simon, one of Wolfe Tone's confidants aboard the Hoche was interviewed by Lord Cavan for several hours during which time he gave a full account of the purpose and planning of the expedition. Wolfe Tone expected to be treated as a prisoner of war, being a general in the French Army. When Lord Cavan refused to extend him this privilege, Wolfe Tone wrote to Lord Castlereagh, saying that the Honour of the French Nation was being impugned by his treatment. Lord Castlereagh did not reply. General Hardy wrote to Lord Cornwallis complaining that Wolfe Tone was being treated like a common criminal. Lord Cornwallis's secretary replied saying that " Wolfe Tone is known only to his excellency as a traitor." At this time Lord Cornwallis was being criticised by the Dublin Government as being too lenient with the prisoners. When Tone arrived in Dublin he was a dressed in the full regalia of a French general complete with a powder blue uniform laced gold trimmings a cocked hat and gold epaulets. He travelled through the city along the north quays and passed the newly completed Four Courts. He was lodged in the Provost Prison in the Royal Barracks where his brother had been held some weeks earlier.

Russell and Neilson were still in Newgate and Emmet and McNevin were in Kilmainham jail.

Wolfe Tone was tried in the Barracks by a military court of seven officers on the 10th of November. He was charged with high treason. When the charges were read out he asked to address the court in order to explain his actions. After a discussion by the officers he was allowed to read from a prepared paper and he addressed the court as follows ;

" Mr. President and gentlemen of the Court Martial. It is not my intent to give the Court any trouble; I admit the charge against me in the fullest extent; what I have done, I have done and I am prepared to stand the consequences.

The great object of my life has been the independence of my country ; for that I have sacrificed everything that is most dear to man; placed in an honourable poverty I have more than once rejected offers considerable to a man in my circumstances, where the condition expected was in opposition to my principles; for them I have braved difficulty and danger: I have submitted to exile and to bondage; I have exposed myself to the rage of the Ocean and the fire of the enemy; after an honourable combat that should have interested the feelings of a generous foe, I have been marched through the country in irons to the disgrace alone of whoever gave the order; I have devoted even my wife and children; after that last effort it is little to say that I am ready to lay down my life.

Whatever I have said, written or thought on the subject of Ireland I now reiterate: looking upon the connection with England to have been her bane I have endeavoured by every means in my power to break that connexion; I have laboured in consequence to create a people in Ireland by raising three millions of my countrymen to the rank of citizens.

Having considered the resources of this Country and satisfied that she was too weak to assert her liberty by her own proper means, I sought assistance where I thought assistance was to be found; I have been in consequence in France where without

*patron or protector, without art or intrigue I have had the
honour to be adopted as a Citizen and advanced to a superior
rank in the armies of the Republic; I have had the confidence of
the French Government. the approbation of my Generals and the
esteem of my brave comrades; It is not the sentence of the Court
however I may personally respect the members who compose it
that can destroy the consolation I feel from these considerations.
Such are my principles such has been my conduct; if in
consequence of the measures in which I have been engaged
misfortunes have been brought upon this country, I heartily
lament it, but let it be remembered that it is now nearly four
years since I have quitted Ireland and consequently I have been
personally concerned in non of them; if I am rightly informed
very great atrocities have been committed on both sides, but that
does not at all diminish my regret; for a fair and open war I was
prepared; if that has degenerated into a system of assassination,
massacre and plunder I do again most sincerely lament it, and
those few who know me personally will give me I am sure the
credit for the assertion. I will not detain you longer; in this world
success is everything; I have attempted to follow the same line in
which Washington succeeded and Kosciusko failed; I have
attempted to establish the independence of my country; I have
failed in the attempt; my life is in consequence forfeited and I
submit the Court will do their duty and I shall endeavour to do
mine.3*

When Wolfe Tone was finished speaking he was asked if he had
anything further to say. He asked that he be executed by firing
squad as befits the death of a soldier. Tone one knew he would be
condemned to be executed so he refused to see his friends or
family. He wrote to the prisoners in Kilmainham on the
afternoon of his trial and asked them to take care of his family.
He also wrote a final letter to his wife Matilda in which he says;

*" The hour is at last come, when we must part; as no words can
express what I feel for you and our children, I shall not attempt
it; complaint of any kind would be beneath your courage and
mine. "*

Wolfe Tone was told on Sunday evening the 11th of November that he was to be hanged publicly at Newgate prison at 1.pm the following day at the request of the members of Dublin Corporation. However, Lord Cornwallis remitted that part of the sentence which required his head to be struck off and fixed on a spike. At 4 a.m. on Monday morning Wolfe Tone was found in a pool of blood with his throat cut. A Surgeon was sent for and the wound was sewn up. The wound was described as serious but not fatal. Later that morning an attempt was made to overturn the trial by claiming that the court martial was illegal. Arthur Wolfe the presiding judge ordered the sheriff to go the Barracks and have the execution postponed. The sheriff was not allowed to enter the Barracks but he returned that with the news that Wolfe Tone had attempted suicide. They were also told that it would be four days before they would know for sure if the wound was fatal. The newspapers reported that Wolfe Tone could not be moved because the slightest movement would kill him. It was also said that he was held in a straight jacket to prevent him from making further suicide attempts. Wolfe Tone's condition deteriorated over the course of a week and he died on the 19th of November 1798. Lord Castlereagh gave permission for Wolfe Tone's Body to be taken by his friends. His remains were removed to the home of the Dunbavins of High Street. For two days mourners visited the house to pay their respects. On the 21st of November his remains were finally removed to Bodenstown where he was buried in a private ceremony as by Government order.

Conclusion

" Wolfe Tone was a most extraordinary man and his history is the most curious history of those times. With a hundred guineas in his pocket, unknown and unrecommended he went to Paris in order to overturn the British Government in Ireland. "4 So said the Duke of Wellington. Considering his adversaries accord him so much respect, no impartial observer could offer him less.

Wolfe Tone was a child of privilege but he never wielded power within the Irish Ascendancy. He held the Irish Parliament in contempt, but is difficult to be sure where his contempt originated. His admiration for the French clearly grew out of their military prowess. His anxiety to be a soldier was gratified by the French but it might just as easily have been gratified by the British had Mr. Pitt taken more account of his Hawaiian proposals. Wolfe Tone's political evolution was clearly driven by the events of his time. His advocacy of the Catholic cause was a lot more than a commercial enterprise, but his association with the Catholic Committee would have induced him to be more conservative rather than less. It was his association with the radicals of Belfast that spurred him to examine republican ideals and it was his ability as a polemicist that gained him influence with Catholic and Dissenters alike. His closest friend was Thomas Russell, but his relationship with the other leaders of the '98 Rebellion is difficult to evaluate. He disliked Tandy and seemed to be in conflict with Lord Edward on certain points. James Hope whose autobiography is among the most comprehensive from that time fails to mention Wolfe Tone from beginning to end. However, Hope repeatedly condemns those who hazarded all on foreign aid. It is quite clear that the Revolution was originally planned for February '98 but was postponed in the hope of foreign assistance. On the other hand it is quite clear that Tone and Lewins expected the arrival of the French troops to act as a signal for the rising. But even if these misunderstandings had been successfully ironed out, Wolfe Tone still had the weather to contend with. Napoleon said, in another context, " give me generals who are lucky." Wolfe Tone was surely the unluckiest general that Napoleon ever had!

end

HenryJoy
McCracken

Henry Joy McCracken

HENRY JOY McCRACKEN
1767-1798

HenryJoy McCracken led his men into battle on the 7th of June 1798. On that day Lord Edward was dead. Wolfe Tone, James Tandy, Hamilton Rowan and Edward Lewins were in Paris. Thomas Russell, Samuel Neilson, Thomas Emmet Arthur O'Connor, John and Henry Sheares, William Byrne, Oliver Bond, John McCann, Richard McCormick and William McNevin were all in prison. Simms, Sinclair and Hunter had all resigned on the eve of Battle. Wicklow, Wexford, Carlow and Kildare had already risen, and every where the rebels were under pressure. As commander of the United Army of Ulster, HenryJoy knew, that his would be the last throw of the dice.

Unlike Russell, Neilson and Tone, HenryJoy McCracken left no large body of writings behind him through which we can trawl, to judge his motives, scrutinise his convictions or analyse his philosophy. Such is the cause of his obscurity. Anecdotes tell us that he set up a Sunday school, and a lending library, that he fought fires and was good with machinery. His concern for the poor is better documented but there is a tendency when so little is known to focus on every detail and magnify it to a point where the whole picture becomes distorted. There is also a tendency to digress into tangential biographies which dwarf the subject and cloud the salient facts. HenryJoy McCracken, man of courage deserves better.

HenryJoy McCracken was born in Belfast on the 31st of August 1767. His father was a retired sea captain who founded the Sea Man's Mission and also established the first rope walk on the quays of Belfast. His mother had her own muslin business which was highly successful and profitable. His grandfather Francis Joy founded the Belfast Newsletter and established the first major paper making company in Ireland. HenryJoy had four brothers and two sisters all of whom were successfully engaged in the cotton and textile business in Belfast. His uncles Henry Joy Sen. and Robert Joy were mainly responsible for the building of the Belfast Poor House. He also had two cousins both of whom were called Henry Joy, one the proprietor of the Belfast Newsletter and the other a barrister in Dublin.

HenryJoy received his education at a private school in Belfast run by Mr. David Mason who thought in a liberal and progressive manner. Little is known about his academic achievements other than that he could read French. He started work in the family business at seventeen as a junior manager and general maintenance man. At 22 years old he was made general manager of Joy McCabe and McCracken and he went to Scotland to recruit skilled workers for their cotton mill which was newly established at the Falls outside Belfast. In 1788 HenryJoy and sister MaryAnn set-up a Sunday school in the local Market House where adults as well as children could learn to read and write. As this was open to all denominations it soon came under suspicion and was closed down by order of the Town Sovereign. HenryJoy then established a cheap lending library where the poor could obtain access to a wide range of popular books. HenryJoy's older brothers William and Francis were members of the Volunteers. They were present when the 1st company of the Belfast Volunteers paraded as mark of respect at the opening of the first Catholic Chapel in Belfast in 1784. This was the same year that the Belfast Volunteers invited into their ranks " persons of every religious persuasion, firmly convinced that a general union of all the inhabitants of Ireland is as necessary to the freedom and prosperity of this Kingdom, as it is congenial to the constitution." This shows the degree of flexibility and co-operation that existed between the Presbyterians and Catholics of Belfast even before 1790. The McCrackens employed Catholics within their household so their ecumenical spirit was well established before Wolfe Tone's "Argument on Behalf of Catholics." The Volunteers which had been established in 1778 had begun to decline to a point where special efforts were being made to revive them in 1792. At the beginning of that year a meeting was held in Belfast at the 3rd Congregational Hall to discuss the position of Catholics. After some discussion the following resolution was passed.

*" We pray that the legislature may be pleased to repeal all penal and restrictive statutes at present in existence against the Roman Catholics; and that they may be restored to the rank and consequence of citizens. "*1

Prominent at these events were Francis and William McCracken with HenryJoy   deferring to his older brothers. However HenryJoy's cousin Henry Joy (the Belfast Newsletter) used his newspaper to express his reservations and he demanded that the Catholic Hierarchy should be obliged to declare their Loyalty to the King before such rights were accorded to them. These differing emphasises made the whole topic of Catholic emancipation a live issue in Belfast at that time. Towards the end of 1790 Thomas Russell arrived in Belfast to take up his commission in the 64th Regiment of Foot. He was born in the same year as HenryJoy, and when the two met they quickly became   firm friends. Russell was interested in the work of Edward Bunting who was an excellent musician, and a collector of ancient Irish harp music. Bunting had been resident in the McCracken household since his early boyhood. HenryJoy's circle of friends in 1791 therefore included Thomas Russell, Edward Bunting, Samuel Neilson, Robert and William Simms, John Templeton, Samuel McTier, William Sinclair and the Rev. Sinclair Kelburne. Both the McCracken's and the Templeton's were famous for their hospitality and HenryJoy "delighted in organising a good party." McCracken was often away from home taking care of the family business and MaryAnn noted that HenryJoy's presence was " essential to the success of any social occasion."

A major celebration of Bastille Day was planned for the 14th of July 1792 and Wolfe Tone was invited to Belfast to present his address to the People of Ireland. Wolfe Tone also, was warmly welcomed into the McCracken household. Neilson, Russell and Wolfe Tone launched their United Irish Society in 1792 but HenryJoy continued to play party host and tend to his textile business at the falls. He became more and more familiar with the rural poor and it was with them that most of his concerns lay. While Thomas Russell and Wolfe Tone journeyed back and forth between Dublin and Belfast, HenryJoy set-up a calico printing works at Knockaird. Wolfe Tone visited McCracken's works on one occasion and was sufficiently impressed to remark upon it favourably in his diary. Unfortunately, HenryJoy did not keep a diary, and indeed was reluctant to write letters even while in prison. In 1791 Thomas Paine published his book the "Rights of Man". We have no opinions on this from HenryJoy, but he might have been influenced by it for we know from MaryAnn McCracken, that it was discussed in depth in the McCracken household and Wolfe Tone described it as the "Koran of Belfastcu". Meanwhile Neilson and Russell were spreading the gospel of the United Irishmen throughout the north of Ireland. They were gradually overcoming the divisions between the Defenders (Catholics) and the Peep-o-Day Boys (Protestants).In Dublin Wolfe Tone had organised the National Convention of Catholics. With Wolfe Tone's guidance the Catholics drew up a petition to the King and by 1793 a number of important relief measures for Catholics had been achieved. But also at this time the Government began to introduce measures to curb the political aspirations of the Presbyterians of Belfast. The Insurrection Act, the Arms and Gunpowder Bill and the suppression of the Volunteers were all measures directed against the radicals of Belfast. The Presbyterians of Belfast had already suffered severe damage to their business interests as a result of the wars with America , France and Spain. Unable to trade properly with these other countries, unemployment was growing rapidly throughout the province. Now the Government's clear ambition was to drive a wedge between the Catholics and the Presbyterians by placating one, to a degree, and by repressing the other. At the same time the newly formed militia's who were sent to the north, were deliberately provoking trouble as a pretext to disarming the Volunteers. Meanwhile the recently formed Orange Clubs were engaged in a campaign of sectarian attacks against Catholic families. HenryJoy, seeing this became drawn into the heating up political situation. In Dublin United Irishmen such as Butler and Bond were arrested and held without trial. A House of Lords select Committee engaged in an inquisition in an attempt to blacken the name of the United Irishmen and in an effort to jail and banish it's leading members. James Tandy and Archibald Hamilton Rowan had to flee the country. Even Wolfe Tone himself was banished to America. Because of the Government's illegal and unconstitutional methods the United Irish Society was forced to re-form as a secret society. HenryJoy McCracken was among the first to join the United Irishmen when it was re-modelled in 1795. When Wolfe Tone arrived in Belfast in July 1795 it was HenryJoy McCracken who administered the oath to Wolfe Tone. After their historic meeting on Cave Hill outside Belfast, HenryJoy McCracken joined with Samuel Neilson and Thomas Russell in re-organising the Society on secretive and more militaristic lines. Russell worked in Counties Down, Tyrone and Fermanagh, McCracken worked in Antrim, Armagh Meath and Offaly while Neilson used his paper the "Northern Star" to promote the views of the United Irishmen throughout the country. Around this time also McCracken met James Hope and Charles Teeling. Teeling was a wealthy Catholic linen merchant, and it was with his help that McCracken was able to meet Catholics throughout the province. McCracken used his personal fortune to obtain legal aid for Catholics so that they could fight for compensation when their homes were burned by orange mobs. It was McCracken's main ambition to persuade the Defenders, mostly Catholics, to join the United Irishmen. The Defenders were formed to defend the small holder Roman Catholic farmers and tenants from the onslaughts of their Protestant neighbours in the guise of the Militia and the Yeomen but also as Peep-o-Day Boys. The Defenders were at first opposed to republican ideals and indeed the Roman Catholic clergy were vigorously warning Catholics against republicanism. With Teeling's help McCracken spent from early 1795 until October 1796 organising Catholics into the United Irishmen and he gained their support and respect by taking legal cases on their behalf wherever their property, or persons were attacked by Orangemen, Yeomen or Peep-o-day Boys. In November McCracken and Joseph Cuthbert engaged a solicitor from Belfast to undertake proceedings on behalf of Michael McClooskey, Paul Hannon, Bernard Coil, Patrick Hamill and Sicilly Hamill against John Grier Esq. a magistrate who had failed to vindicate their rights under the law. (Whenever Orangemen or Yeomen were charged with wilful damage or destruction of Catholic property, the Protestant Magistrate would allow them to go scot-free.) It is also recorded that in January '96 McCracken paid £19 to a solicitor named Hartford for

71

representing Catholics whose homes were plundered by Orange mobs. McCracken had plans to engage the assistance of Henry Grattan in his efforts to legally represent Catholics. Consulting with Sampson he went around the country collecting affidavits and engaged in a survey so he could supply Grattan the necessary information. He spent four days from the 2nd to the 6th of January '96 in Lurgan taking depositions from people whose homes had been attacked by Peep-o-day Boys His cousin in Dublin, Councillor Henry Joy, was underwriting his legal expenses at this period. Throughout the rest of the year McCracken toured the country as far afield as Co. Offaly meeting Catholics, representing them and organising them into the United Irishmen. Charles Teeling who was the leader of the Defenders made McCracken a commander within that organisation. McCracken had nearly seven thousand Defenders in his support and nearly all of them joined the United Irishmen.

" The influence of the United Irishmen began to be felt at all public places, fairs, markets, social meetings- extending to all the counties of Ulster, and all who visited Belfast returned promoting the ideas of the United Irishmen. Strife and quarrelling ceased in public places and even drunkenness. "2

Nonetheless, informers continued to operate within the ranks. At the Mudler's Club in Belfast where most of the intelligence between messengers of the United Irishmen was exchanged a notorious informer was at work. McCracken had set up the Club in Barclays' Tavern to co-ordinate counter-espionage. In this he was quite successful as several informers were smoked out. However Belle Martin had caused enormous damage to the Society before her treachery was discovered. While working as a serving girl at the tavern she was all the while selling information to the British. Belle Martin came from Portaferry. Her mother was an invalid and Belle went from house to house begging food and milk. She continued to beg "until she was quiet grown up". Being very good looking she then entered the trade of prostitution. She was charged with lewd conduct but the charges were dropped when she was given protection by Lord Castlereagh. She gave information to Colonel Barber regarding the members of the Monaghan Militia who were also members of the United Irishmen. She went to the Barracks and identified them. They were Daniel Gillian, Peter McCarron and William and Owen McKenna. All four were shot and Lord Edward was moved to tears when he heard of their sacrifice. Belle Martin's treachery was only found out when during a struggle with Peggy Barclay a list fell out of her pocket with the names of the accused on it. She subsequently moved to Dublin where she was provided with an apartment by Lord Castlereagh.

Another informer was Edward Newell. He also identified the soldiers at Blaris Camp and pointed out a further five United Irishmen in Belfast including William McCracken. Newell was a paid agent run by George Murdock who was a heart tax collector in Belfast. Murdock and Newell were living in Dublin Castle waiting to give evidence at the trial of those they had accused. In the meantime a criminal correspondence was discovered between Newell and Murdock's wife. The letters which passed between them was intercepted and James Hope gave them to Murdock. This caused a row between Murdock and Newell. They quarrelled in the Castle yard and Murdock fired a pistol at Newell who then fled to the North taking Murdock's wife with him. Murdock eventually traced Newell and got his wife back but Newell had to flee the country. Another informer operating from Belfast at that time was Thomas Collins who kept the Castle informed about the movements of Thomas Russell. James McGucken a solicitor who acted for HenryJoy and John Hughes who was a close friend of Lord Edward, and who owned a book shop in Belfast where all the United Irishmen used to gather, were also on the government's payroll.

With McCracken travelling all over the country his calico printing business at Knockaird failed. He was absent from Belfast for long periods. Wherever he travelled he noticed a continual increase in repression both from the regular army and from the newly formed militia. Most notoriously the Kerry Militia were feared as they went about the country drunk. The Kerry Militia were Catholics and Irish speakers. They were being used to repress the Presbyterian people of Belfast. An extraordinary development occurred when the Kerry Militia were attacked by the Orangemen and the Yeomen even though they were all on the

Government's side! Nine of the Kerry militia were killed in the skirmish.

Meanwhile Lord Castlereagh, an erstwhile friend of Samuel Neilson, who was a nephew of the Viceroy Lord Camden, had become a particular favourite of Mr. Pitt the British Prime Minister. He fully supported Mr. Pitt's plan to bring about a legislative union between the parliaments of Britain and Ireland. Lord Castlereagh was fully briefed on the information being received by the Castle about the activities of the United Irishmen. He decided to " cut the head off the monster " and he believed that the head was in Belfast. On the 16th of September 1796 Lord Castlereagh with the support of Lord Downshire and Lord Westmeath and accompanied by a large force of cavalry entered Belfast and commenced a widespread search for the leaders of the United Irishmen. Neither Russell or Neilson were in hiding and they soon surrendered to Castlereagh expecting a quick trial and early release. Twelve prisoners in all were arrested among them Charles Teeling, and all were taken to Dublin each in a separate carriage and all surrounded by cavalry. The prisoners were cheered by large crowds as they left Belfast, so dense that it was difficult for the cavalcade to get through. The cavalcade stopped at Newry to rest and feed the horses and the local people climbed under the bellies of the horses to bring food and drink to the prisoners. When they reached Dublin the Castle was in darkness as they were totally unexpected. They were then divided into two groups one going to Newgate and the other going to Kilmainham. Meanwhile HenryJoy was still at large and continuing his work in the country areas. An around the clock watch was put on his house and Belfast officials were greatly frustrated by his failure to return. However after much vigilance McCracken and his friend Thomas Richardson were arrested in Armagh on the 10th of October. They were brought to Dublin by coach and engaged in lively discussion with their captors, not all of whom were opposed to the views of the United Irishmen. Initially they were both held in Newgate, which was an old and dirty prison, where Thomas Russell and some of the other state prisoners were still held. After some days McCracken was moved to Kilmainham where he was kept in solitary confinement. McCracken who was tall and thin suffered from rheumatism and this was immediately aggravated by the prison conditions. The governor of the prison however, was a humane man and he treated the prisoners with courtesy and discretion.

HenryJoy's sisters MaryAnn and Margaret travelled to Dublin immediately to visit their brother. When they entered the prison they found their brother who they always referred to as Harry, in a dark, dank and must-smelling cell with the chill already affecting his bones. McCracken however just smiled and wanted to know what was happening in the North.

The news was not good, as they told of the increased beatings and torture which were daily taking place throughout the province. The sisters were permitted to bring in food and clothes but not writing materials or newspapers. Although McCracken was allowed to receive letters, which were first read by the Governor, he was not allowed to write out.

After a few weeks the prisoners were allowed to associate more freely within the prison. The McCracken sisters who remained in Dublin for several weeks, stayed at the home of their cousin, Councillor Joy who lived at Temple street. A Catholic merchant named Dixon who lived near Kilmainham gave shelter to the wives of Neilson and Haslett and the relatives of several of the other prisoners stayed in the home of Oliver Bond in Bridge Street. Throughout their stay in prison the prisoners continued to get news of the repression being carried on outside.

In a letter to HenryJoy his brother John gave this as his experience;

" For some time past I have been loitering my time at Moneymore, where an opportunity of writing to you was not to be found, and I had nothing to tell you of except the barbarities committed on the innocent country people by the yeomen and Orangemen. The practice among them is to hang a man up by the heels with a rope of full twist, by which means the sufferer whirls round like a bird roasting at the fire, during which he is lashed with belts, etc., to make him tell where arms are concealed. Last week, at a place near Dungannon, a young man *being used in this manner called to his father for assistance, who being inflamed at the sight, struck one of the party a desperate blow with his turf spade; but alas! his life paid the forfeit of his rashness: his entrails were torn out and exposed on a torn bush. "*

*" This is but one barbarity of the many which are daily practised about the county Tyrone and Armagh; however the county Antrim is not so bad, but I believe not much better. "*3

Meanwhile the prisoners occupied themselves by reading and playing football. HenryJoy's choice was Caleb Williams by the French writer Godwin. Most educated citizens were fascinated by the French at this time. As Christmas approached Oliver Bond's wife got permission from the governor to bake the prisoners a large pie for Christmas day. Governor's wife was presented with a similar but smaller pie, while the Governor received a gift of cash. When the prisoners opened their pie on Christmas day they found the base of it packed with writing materials and newspapers. Charles Teeling says that this was the single most uplifting occurrence during their stay in prison.

Lord Castlereagh also visited the prison. He had a private audience with Samuel Neilson. Neilson asked Lord Castlereagh to reprieve two prisoners who were under sentence of death. Castlereagh agreed and soon after the two prisoners were released. However Neilson's private discussions caused friction within the prison. For some months several of the prisoners refused to speak to Neilson. Neilson wrote a poem to express his isolation at this period.

The subtle moon since I came here
Revolving had fulfilled her year
A year not long tis true to spend
At liberty and with many a friend
But in these dreary walls enclosed
Fretted at heart and much abused
Assailed by every babbling tongue
*One year appears a hundred long.*4

HenryJoy McCracken was one of those critical of Neilson at this time but after the intervention of his sister MaryAnn, harmony was restored. However while the prisoners were enjoying their Christmas pie in Kilmainham, Wolfe Tone was being battered by high winds off the coast of county Cork. When the invasion force failed to land the British were given a vital breathing space. The repression which had formerly been concentrated in the North was now spread throughout the rest of the country. Torture chambers were set up in Dublin in the Old Custom House, in Beresford Riding school and Sandy's Provost. One man was seen running from the torture chambers at the Old Custom House, his body in flames. He jumped into the Liffey and drowned rather face further torture. Another prisoner was lashed to death with a cat-o-nine tails for wearing a ring with clasped hands, the symbol of the United Irishmen. A third man in Drogheda was sentenced to 500 lashes and after the first few lashes he agreed to give information about hidden arms. When he was released he cut his own throat rather than give the information.

With all the Northern leaders in prison, the organisation of the Society was left to the Leinster Directory. James Hope who had been helpful to HenryJoy in organising the North came to Dublin to help organise the working class people of the Liberties. He was very successful and within a short time there were two thousand United Irishmen in Dublin city and a further three thousand in the county area. Lord Edward Fitzgerald was appointed the Commander-in-Chief of the United Irish Army in the Spring of 1797. He sent emissaries to France seeking immediate aid for a rising of the people. Lord Edward was coming under pressure from the people of the North who were still suffering the worst of the repression. Lord Edward entered Kilmainham Jail in the middle of '97 to meet McCracken and Neilson. The organisation and preparation of the province were only fully known to Neilson and McCracken. The prison governor's wife allowed Lord Edward access to the prison and she warned him when the Governor returned unexpectedly. Lord Edward, who was in disguise was forced to remain in the cell of Charles Teeling overnight until the governor's wife allowed him to leave the following morning.

HenryJoy's brother William was also held at Kilmainham and they were joined on later occasions by Rev. Kelburne and Dr. Crawford. HenryJoy was eventually able to write letters from Kilmainham and in all he wrote eight letters while a prisoner there. Most his letters were concerned with living conditions at the prison and the relationships between the prisoners. He was most concerned that the poorer prisoners could not afford to have food and clothing sent in and in one letter he says;

*" It is expensive to live here plundered by the turnkeys, etc. and still more so when confined with others who cannot support themselves and yet cannot be left to themselves. "*5

He was at all times taken up with the plight of his fellow prisoners as evidenced by another letter where he says;

*" Yesterday two men were hanged in front of the jail for robbing the Mail in June last, they died with the greatest fortitude. One of them going past our window for execution turned round and saluted us with the greatest composure. It gives me a carelessness about death to see such sights. "*6

In April of '97 HenryJoy was reduced from the rank of State prisoner to that of common felon. This meant that he had greater freedom within the jail. The governors wife allowed the prisoners to use the kitchen and to cook their own food and they took turns at cooking, some being better cooks than others. Kilmainham was a newer and cleaner prison than Newgate, but it was more secure and access was more restricted. Thomas Russell was never to join his friend HenryJoy at Kilmainham but remained in Newgate until 1799. In the autumn of 1797 Lord Edward sent Colonel James Plunket and William Putnam McCabe to the north to see if preparations there were advanced enough to commence the rising, but after a false alarm they returned to Dublin without adequate information and declared that the North was not ready. Meanwhile William McCracken became seriously ill and his wife came to Dublin and stayed with at Kilmainham in an effort to nurse him back to health. HenryJoy's rheumatism had improved over the summer months but as the weather worsened he was in great pain again. None of the prisoners had been placed on trial except William Orr. When he was convicted and executed the United Irishmen went into a spasm of grief. Numerous letters of condemnation were printed by Arthur O'Connor in his newspaper "The Press". To show their support, hundreds of people went to the homes and farms of the prisoners and helped to save their crops. William Orr's field of hay was cut, baled and saved in one hour. Samuel Neilson's field of potatoes was dug up, bagged and stored in " seven minutes."

After persistent representations on their behalf by Councillor Joy, HenryJoy and his brother William were released on bail on the 8th of December 1797. In the hours before they left prison the had to find money to pay doctors, legal fees and to repay the governor's wife who had loaned them money and been of great assistance on numerous occasions during their captivity. As soon as he was free William returned to the North but HenryJoy stayed in Dublin for a few days to thank those, such as Mr. Dixon for their help and to visit Russell in Newgate. Nevertheless McCracken was back in Belfast for Christmas and he spent the next six weeks rebuilding his health which had deteriorated badly over the winter.

HenryJoy was back in Dublin again by February. He joined Lord Edward and Samuel Neilson at the National Convention of United Irish Delegates held in The Shakespeare Gallery in Exchange Street on the 26th of February 1798. Lord Edward had just sent Arthur O'Connor and Fr. Quigley to France to re-establish contacts with the French after the British had intercepted previous letters and interrupted their communications. At the convention all the Northern delegates were in favour of an immediate rising. HenryJoy said that he had 7000 men in Antrim who would " *rather be in the field like men, than hunted like wild beasts, and see their friends carried off to jail, their houses ransacked and the cowardly yeomen riding roughshod over them day by day.*"7
This call to arms was supported by delegates from Derry, Down, Wicklow Wexford, Meath and Carlow. However the delegates from Connaught failed to arrive at the convention and the delegates from Dublin were opposed to an early rising. Thomas Emmet and William McNevin spoke against it saying that

*"success was improbable without French aid and our middle ranking officers had no military experience or training."*8

Lord Edward said that *" We have overwhelming numbers and the element of surprise. The Capital can be taken easily. Are we not prepared to free our country unless the French come?" "If 5000 is not enough how may would be enough?"*9

Lord Edward presented a report which set out the strength of the organisation and it's finances in the different counties.

County	Men	Cash in Hand
Ulster	110,000	£436 2s 4d
Munster	100,634	£147 19s 2d
Kildare	10,863	£110 17s 7d
Wicklow	12,895	£ 93 6s 4d
Dublin	3,010	£ 37 2s 6d
Dublin Co.	2,177	£ 321 17s 11d
Queen's Co.	11,689	£ 91 2s 1d
King's Co.	3,600	£ 21 11s 3d
Carlow	9,414	£ 49 2s 10d
Kilkenny	624	£ 10 2s 3d
Meath	1,400	£ 171 2s 0d
Total	**279896**	**Total £ 1,485 4s 9d**

This report was prepared by Lord Edward and written out in his own handwriting. A copy of it was made by Thomas Reynolds and handed to Dublin Castle.

William McNevin said that *" even if all these men had signed up, there was no guarantee that they would fight. Many did not know what they had signed up for."*10

After much heated discussion the following resolutions were passed.

*" That we pay no attention whatever to any attempts by either
house of Parliament to divert the public mind from the course
we have in view, as nothing short of immediate emancipation of
our country will satisfy us. "*

*" That the counties of Carlow, Meath, Wicklow, Derry, Down
and Antrim deserve well of their country for their manly offer
emancipating her directly; but that they be requested to bear the
shackles of tyranny a little longer: until the whole Kingdom shall
be in such a state of organisation as will by their joint co-
operation effect without loss their desirable point: which is
hourly being accomplished and will tend most expeditiously to
bring about a union of the four provinces, three only having, as
yet come forward. "*11

The convention broke up without setting a date for the rising.
With so many spies in Dublin, the fact that the convention had
taken place could not have been kept secret for long. O'Connor
and Quigley were arrested at Margate on their way to France.
With this news Lord Edward knew that French aid might be
postponed indefinitely. With the arrest of O'Connor, Dublin was
now isolated from Paris. When the Leinster Directory were
arrested on the 12th of March, barely a fortnight after the
convention, it was obvious that the Government had enough
information to strangle the United Irishmen. On the 30th of
March the country was declared to be in a state of " Actual
Rebellion." When John and Henry Sheares were appointed to
replace the Leinster Directors now in prison, the balance of
opinion fell in favour of an immediate rising. Lord Edward went
into hiding in Dublin and was soon in contact with all the
leading figures within the Society. When the decision to launch
the rising on the 23rd of May was taken, Lord Edward, Samuel
Neilson, HenryJoy McCracken, the Sheares brothers and James
Plunket were free and active in Dublin. McCracken returned to
Belfast in the middle of May leaving the capture of the capital to
Lord Edward, Neilson and the Sheares brothers. Lord Edward
and Neilson met with their officers including James Plunket the
commander for Connaught to finalise the plans for the crucial
day. HenryJoy brought the instructions to the commander for the
North, Robert Simms. James Hope was appointed Aid-de-Camp

to Robert Simms and he returned to Belfast as per instructions. On the 19th of May Lord Edward was arrested while resting in his room in a house in Thomas Street. Two days later John and Henry Sheares were arrested while going about their business in the city. On 23rd of May Samuel Neilson was arrested while trying to effect the escape of the prisoners in Newgate prison. On the evening of the 23rd of May the Mail coaches entering Dublin were overturned and burned. In the early hours of the 24th of May the rising commenced with an attack on the Militia barracks at Naas. One thousand rebels mostly armed with pikes laid siege to the Barracks at 1am. However information had been received and the barracks with 400 soldiers and 100 cavalry was well prepared by the commander Lord Gosford. The rebels were met with a constant hail of musket fire. Unable to press home their attack the rebels withdrew and were pursued by the waiting cavalry who cut them down as they retreated. As many as one hundred rebels were killed in this first engagement against a loss of fifty soldiers and two officers. Later that day rebel attacks took place at Baltinglass, Ballymore Eustace, Prosperous, Clare, Kilcullen , Monastereven, Carlow and Dunboyne. In all twenty three battles had been fought by the 5th of June 1798.

The North

When HenryJoy returned to Belfast in May 1798 the newspapers were full of reports of the trial of Arthur O'Connor and Fr. Quigley. When the news of the arrests of the Leinster Directory came through the Northern Executive went into a state of shock. HenryJoy brought the orders form the Commander-in-Chief, Lord Edward, that the rising was to start everywhere on 23rd of May. At a meeting of the Northern Executive, HenryJoy proposed that the Commanding Officers for Belfast should be kidnapped while attending a Musical Concert which was to be held in the Assembly Rooms on May 21st. Two members of the executive, Samuel Neilson and Oliver Bond were absent from the meeting, being detained in Newgate prison. McCracken's proposal was over-ruled by the other members of the executive. Robert Simms the Commander for Antrim asked for time to organise his plans and his troops. James Hope, who was his aid-de-camp, was to

carry Simms's instructions to the other officers. Speaking of this
period James Hope says;

" *The idea of foreign aid, and the French connection, which*
although the original projectors of the society did not approve
of, was now introduced by men of weight and influence in the
societies. HenryJoy McCracken was the first who observed the
design and operation of this under plot. The majority of the
leaders became foreign aid men, and were easily elevated or
depressed by the news from France, and amongst their ranks,
spies were chiefly found. They were also the prolific source of
contradictory rumours, to distract the societies and paralyse
confidence. The appearance of a French fleet in Bantry Bay,
brought the rich farmers and shop keepers into the societies, and
with them all the corruption essential to the objects of the British
ministry, to foster rebellion, to possess the power of subduing it
and to carry a legislative Union. The new adherents alleged as a
reason for their former reserve, that they thought the societies,
only a combination of the poor to get the property of the rich.
The societies, as a mark of satisfaction at their conversion, and
in demonstration of confidence in their wealthy associates, the
future leaders, civil and military, were chiefly chosen from their
ranks. McCracken, who was by far the most deserving of all our
leaders, observed that "what we had latterly gained in numbers
we lost in worth" He foresaw that the corruption of Ulster would
*endanger the union in the south. "*12

After some days of inaction, Hope requested instructions from
Simms. Simms sent Hope to Dunboyne to see if there was a rebel
army assembled there. Along the way Hope met McCracken and
explained his mission saying he was afraid to disobey Simms in
case he was court-marshalled. McCracken suspected that Simms
was disobeying the order to rise and said that " *there is no army*
at Dunboyne and the men at Tara have already been defeated."
McCracken ordered Hope to return to Belfast and he confronted
Simms who resigned as did Robert Hunter the Commander for
Down. John Coulter and Henry Munro were appointed to replace
them. HenryJoy however, became provisional commander
pending contact with the new colonels. When neither could be
contacted McCracken sent Hope with messages to George

Sinclair and Rev. Steele Dickson who were also members of the Northern executive. Sinclair also resigned and the letter to Dickson was torn up by the wife of one of the United Irishmen. Dickson was subsequently arrested on his way to the rendezvous. There was much confusion and not a little recrimination. Simms and Hunter resigned on the 1st of June. By the 4th of June HenryJoy was commander of the United Army of Ulster. He had three days to make his plans.

McCrackens Plans

HenryJoy assumed his responsibilities on the day that Lord Edward died. He knew that Dublin had not been taken. But he also knew that the rebels were in control of much of Wexford. He also knew that the Wexford men had already tried to break through to the North. All over the country the rebels were still fighting with pikes, while Ulster was the only province where the rebels had access to large quantities of fire arms. He also knew that death was certain for all those leaders now in enemy prisons. In view of the failure in Dublin McCracken decided to avoid a direct assault on Belfast. He would launch joint and simultaneous attacks in Antrim and Down thereby dividing Crown forces. This also meant that his men had a shorter distance to travel to the battle. Each colonel with 500 men was to capture the nearest military post and cut it off by leaving armed parties to stop communications. Randlestown, Ballynahinch, Saintfield, Newtownards and Portaferry were the main targets. They were then to assemble on Donegore Hill. Meanwhile McCracken himself was to assemble the men of Killead, Templepatrick, Carnmoney and Donegore and lead them all into Antrim. McCracken sent these written and signed instructions to each of his officers. He chose the 7th of June as the date for the rising because Lord O'Neil was hosting a meeting for all the county magistrates in Antrim town on that day. He proposed to capture the magistrates and use them as bargaining counters, possibly in exchange for the lives of the imprisoned leaders. McCracken sent James Hope to retrieve muskets, gunpowder and musket balls from where there were stored in Belfast.

McCracken's Difficulties

The resignation of the Colonels on the eve of Battle undermined all likelihood of success. The ordinary foot soldiers of the United Irishmen were not inspired by the sight of their leaders turning tail at the last moment. McCracken was further hampered by the most extraordinary treachery. His officers in Larne, Broughshane and Loughguile had all handed their written instructions directly to the local British commanders. McCracken finalised his plans at mid-night on the 6th of June. Within an hour the Plans had reached General Nugent. HenryJoy McCracken had been steadfast in his opposition to the assassination of informers. Informers had regularly been drowned in Dublin, where James Hope had a narrow escape. Informers were also drowned in Wexford. General Lake had promised " *inviolable secrecy* " to informers and the Government had postponed numerous trials indefinitely, rather expose their informants to danger. On the eve of the battle the lives of hundreds of his men had already been sold by those whom McCracken had naively protected.

When General Nugent received his information about rebel intentions he sent instructions to Blaris Camp that the Second Light Battalion consisting of;

1) The 64th Regiment of Foot
2) The Kerry Militia
3) The Dublin Militia
4) The Tipperary Militia
5) The Armagh Militia
6) The Monaghan Militia
7) 150 of the 22nd Lt. Dragoons

plus two cannon and two five inch Howitzer guns

was to march to Antrim as soon as possible.

He also ordered 250 of the Monaghan Militia, a troop of the 2nd Lt. Dragoons and The Belfast Cavalry to march to Antrim via Carnmoney and Templepatrick. The first was under the command of Colonel Clavering and the second under the Command of Colonel Lumley. He also sent a despatch to Major

85

Seddon in Antrim to warn him of the attack and advise him that reinforcements were on the way. By 9 am. on the 7th of June the orderlies had arrived in Antrim but there was no sign of action. In all General Nugent had committed 3000 men to the battle.

The Battle

HenryJoy McCracken and James Hope arrived at Craigarogan early on the summer morning of June 7th. They were quickly joined by about 80 of their comrades from the surrounding district. McCracken had 21,000 men signed up for the rising but it was never part of his plan to assemble them all in one place and march them all across the province. Nevertheless, even at this early stage there was disappointment that all who were committed had not turned up.

McCracken addressed his followers and said;

*" If we succeed today there will be sufficient praise lavished on us, if we fail we may expect proportionate blame! But whether we succeed or fail, let us try to deserve success."*13

Speaking afterwards about McCracken's attitude on that morning, James Hope said ;

*" HenryJoy had no other intention in making the attempt, than to try this last effort of effecting a junction with the men in arms in the South, to gain that point, he was quite willing to sacrifice his life."*14

At length John McKinney rode up from Carnmoney with the news that large numbers of men were assembling at Killead, Ballyclare and Ballynure. McCracken unfurled his green banner, lined his men up and marched towards Antrim. In this his first contingent he had 18 musketeers and 80 pikemen. They had a five mile march to Antrim and all along the way they were joined by men from Carnmoney, Killead, Muckamore and Ballyeaston.

By the time McCracken launched his attack on Antrim his numbers had grown to six and half thousand men.

McCracken's plan was to attack the town from four sides, (1) Belfast road, (2) Carrickfergus road, (3) Pattie's Lane (4) Bow Lane.

Randlestown

The Battle of Randlestown started at 2pm. There were 500 rebels involved and they had fifty muskets but no cannon. The Kings troops had no artillery. The troops shut themselves up in the Barracks and proceeded to fire out the windows at the rebels. The people set fire to the Barracks by piling straw up against the walls. When the fire took hold the soldiers hoisted up a white flag. The rebels put ladders up to the windows and all were taken out and treated with the greatest kindness "none were put to death or offered either injury or insult." The rebels then marched on to meet McCracken at Antrim.

Antrim

The other sections of McCracken's forces converged on Antrim at 2.30pm., coincidentally with the arrival of Colonel Lumley's reinforcements. Lumley's troops succeeded in entering the town by the Masserene Bridge which McCracken had neither the time nor the opportunity to blockade. *" McCracken had no organised staff. All he could do was advise and his forces listened attentively and acted with calm and common sense."* Major Seddon had set many of the houses in the Scotch quarter on fire, and the smoke hampered the rebels as they entered the town. Nevertheless, they entered in good order from the Belfast road until they reached the Presbyterian Meeting House. At this point they were greeted by a party of the 22nd Lt. Dragoons who unleashed a shower of musket fire on their front ranks.

McCracken's men held their ground and the Dragoons were forced to withdraw. McCracken then led his men in a charge to the Churchyard at the crossroads which they captured and there they set up their one piece of cannon. By this time the smoke was operating in the rebels favour as Lumley's musketeers could not find their targets. Lumley ordered his dragoons to charge the rebel position but they were met with a hail of musket fire from the Churchyard and coming within range of the pikemen, 47 of the dragoons were brought down and 40 of the horses killed. Colonel Lumley was injured in the thigh and some of the dragoons fled across the river. McCracken ordered the party which had entered the town from Donegore to proceed to the other side of the town through the back gardens. When the horsemen, still at the market house saw this they made a break for it fearing that they would be surrounded. They made a charge up the Castle road but they too were also brought down by the pikemen. Meanwhile the party trying to enter the town by Bow Lane were prevented from doing so by a continuous volley of fire from the Soldiers behind the Demesne wall. The Victors of Randlestown were just arriving at the Bow Lane entry when the remaining cavalry made a charge through in an effort to escape capture. The Randlestown Victors had not seen any cavalry, nor did they know that the town was in McCracken's control. When they saw the cavalry charge they broke ranks and fled into the fields. When the cavalry saw the disarray, they pressed home their advantage and pursued the fleeing rebels. When Samuel Orr who was commanding the attack on Bow lane, saw the Randlestown men fleeing, he ordered his men to retreat. But this retreat quickly disintegrated into a route. McCracken left James Hope in charge of the contingent in the Church yard while he led a party in an effort to dislodge the soldiers behind Demesne wall. However when his party saw the Bow lane rebels fleeing some of them also broke ranks. McCracken was thrown to the ground by some of his own men as he tried to persuade them to hold fast. He was rescued and protected by John McGivern who finally assured his escape to safety. By this time Colonel Clavering's larger contingent of re-inforcements had arrived and set up their cannon outside the town. After three volleys from his cannon the rebels were seen fleeing the town in every direction. James

Hope's Spartan band were the last to leave the town retreating through Pattie's Lane to Donegore Hill.

Lord O'Neil whom McCracken had targeted as a suitable hostage, was seriously injured during the struggle in Bow Lane. He had fired a pistol at one of the pikemen, who later claimed that he only stabbed O'Neil to protect himself from a second pistol shot. Lord O'Neil died of his wounds four days later.

McCracken's fall-back position was to re-assemble on Donegore Hill. Not all of McCracken's forces were used in the attack on Antrim and a sizeable proportion never entered the town. Some of his troops remained on Donegore throughout the Battle. McCracken had captured George McClaverty at his home that morning. McClaverty was held hostage on Donegore throughout the battle. McClaverty, begged and pleaded with the rebels to cast aside their arms and return to their homes. As a local landowner and Magistrate he promised that he would do all in his power to protect those who abandoned the struggle and returned to their homes. He persuaded 1500 of the 2000 on Donegore to abandon their arms. (He later fulfilled his promise and defended those who had followed his advice.) When the retreating rebels arriving at Donegore heard about the defections, they too lost heart and returned to their homes By now Colonel Clavering's troops had recaptured the town and the fleeing rebels were being slaughtered in the fields. Out of nearly six and a half thousand men McCracken was left with a couple of hundred. Along with his closest supporters McCracken retired to Glenerry where they stayed the night. He was informed in the morning that the men of Kells were still in arms and he set out for Kells. Hope however heard that the rebels from the south were flocking into Ballymena. He went there and met the commander who said that he had 11,000 men. He was planning to march through Armagh and Louth to Dublin. Hope agreed to organise his vanguard. However the entire army dissipated when a rider rode along their ranks saying that " *Lord O'Neil has forgiven everyone a years rent, peace has been declared and the Toomebridge men have accepted it.* "15

McCracken had by then returned from Kells where the rebels had also dispersed. He advised those who were determined not to surrender to repair to Slemish where they could keep a rallying

89

point. They then went to Slemish where McCracken opened a well with his sword so they could have water and they were supplied with food by the local people. They remained on Slemish until Colonel Clavering arrived with 400 men. He sent a message offering a pardon and one hundred guineas each for their leaders, including Samuel Orr, John Orr and Robert Johnstone. HenryJoy was not one on whose head there was a price. McCracken refused the offer and returned a message saying he would pay £400 for the capture of Colonel Clavering. Clavering then threatened to burn every house in the local area if the rebels did not surrender. McCracken then ordered his remaining followers to disperse. They had remained at large for four weeks enjoying the support and protection of the local people and McCracken did not want the people to suffer further on his account. News had reached them of the defeat at Ballynahinch and there seemed little hope of breaking through to the south. MaryAnn McCracken had visited her brother in the mountains bringing him food, money and clothes. She made arrangements for him to escape to America. In his last letter to his sister, written from the Slemish mountains, he wrote;

" *These are the times that try men's souls. You will no doubt hear a great number of things respecting the situation in this country, its present unfortunate state is entirely due to treachery, the rich always betray the poor. In Antrim little or nothing was lost by the people until after the brave men who fought the battle retreated, few of whom fell, not more than 1 for 10 of their enemies, but after the villains who were entrusted with the direction of the lower part of the county gave up, hostages and all, without any cause, private emolument excepted, murder then began and cruelties have continued ever since. It is unfortunate that a few wicked men could thus destroy a county after having been purchased with blood, for it was a fact which I am sure you never knew that on Friday 8th of June all the county was in the hands of the people, Antrim, Belfast and Carrickfergus excepted.*16 Shortly after writing this letter McCracken made his way across the moors to the cottage where his girlfriend Mary Bodle and his daughter Maria lived. Again his sister visited him at this cottage bringing him final details about the escape plans. On the 7th of July McCracken left the cottage in an effort to reach the coast. As he crossed the commons outside

Carrickfergus in the company of his friends Gawin Watt and John Query they were arrested by four yeomen one of whom recognised McCracken. HenryJoy had money bonds on him to the value of £30 which he offered to these yeomen if they were allowed to go free. After some discussion it seemed that the yeomen would accept the bribe and they retired to a public house. However while engaged in discussion one of the yeomen slipped out and returned with soldiers. McCracken and his friends were arrested and quickly lodged in Carrickfergus Jail. That evening, a Sunday, when the McCracken household heard about the arrest MaryAnn and her father set off immediately for Carrickfergus. When they entered the jail they saw where HenryJoy had inscribed the words;

" A friend is worth all the hazard we can run "

McCracken was held in Carrickfergus until the 16th of July when he was brought under heavy escort to Belfast where he was committed to a lockup in the Artillery Barracks. The following day he was tried by court-martial in the exchange building. The proceeding commenced at 12 o'clock with Colonel Montgomery presiding. John Pollock represented the Crown and Thomas Stewart represented McCracken. John Minis and James Beck gave evidence against McCracken. Minis said that HenryJoy had called to his house on the morning of the battle and forced him to come along. He had witnessed the battle and had observed HenryJoy giving orders to the various parties. James Beck said that he saw McCracken taking part in the Battle of Antrim and recognised him by a mark on his neck. At the start of the trial HenryJoy warned his sister that she must be prepared for his conviction. During a break in the trial McCracken was offered his life if he would give information about others involved. He refused. MaryAnn left the trial and went home to inform her mother about how things were going and to get a drink for HenryJoy. In despair Mrs McCracken went to the house of General Nugent to beg for the life of her son. Nugent, who was entering the garden when she arrived, slammed the gate and heaped abuse on Mrs McCracken and on her whole family. When MaryAnn returned the trial was over and HenryJoy had been returned to his cell. He was promptly told that his sentence was to be immediate execution. HenryJoy was astonished, as there was normally one day at least between conviction and execution. McCracken asked to see his pastor Rev Kelburne, but while awaiting the Rev. Kelburne he met with Rev. Steele Dickson who was held at the same prison. McCracken told Rev Dickson that Mary Bodle's child was his and asked that her welfare be taken care of. The Rev. Kelburne, who had been ill in bed, then arrived and broke down crying saying how much he loved HenryJoy. MaryAnn McCracken described the last hours of her brother's life thus.

*" About 5pm. he was ordered to the place of execution, the old market-house, the ground of which of which had been given to the town by his great-great-grandfather. I took his arm, and we walked together to the place of execution, where I was told that it was the General's orders that I should leave him which I peremptorily refused . Harry begged I should go. clasping my hands around him, I said I could bear any thing but leaving him. Three times he kissed me, and entreated I would go; and looking round to recognise some friend to put me in charge of, he beckoned to a Mr. Boyd and said " He will take charge of you" Mr. Boyd stepped forward: and fearing any further refusal would disturb the last moments of my dearest brother, I suffered myself to be led away."*17

John Smith who was a young boy present at the execution of McCracken describes what followed.

*" He had a calm serene countenance on which the prospect of death seemed to shed the radiance of glory. He stood for a moment beneath the gallows, his eyes following the retreating figure of his devoted sister. He then turned his gaze upon the crowd, and seemed as if he would address them. Hoarse orders were given by the officers, the troops moved about, the people murmured, a horrible confusion ensued, and in a minute or so the manly, handsome figure on which the impression of nobility was stamped, was dangling at the rope's end. The body was soon cut down, the only favour extended to it was freedom from mutilation.*18

The Freeman's Journal of July 19th carried this report;

Tuesday last, one McCracken was executed at Belfast for High Treason. He had been confined in this city for seditious charges, but his escape from punishment operated as an encouragement instead of a warning.19

McCracken's body was given to his family on condition that he was buried quickly and without ceremony. He was buried in the old graveyard at the end of High street. The graveyard was subsequently built over but when the buildings built thereon, were being demolished, the bones of HenryJoy were recovered and re-interred in the grave of his sister MaryAnn in the Clifton Street cemetery.

Neither Russell, Neilson or Tone ever expressed sadness or sorrow at the news of HenryJoy's death. HenryJoy's last words to his sister MaryAnn were; *" tell Russell I did my duty "* but no reply came. Not a word of admiration for his unparalleled courage, came from these three closest friends, or is recorded in their voluminous letters, journals and diaries. Neither did any of the three utter a syllable in criticism of the conduct of Simms, Hunter or Sinclair whose actions most certainly plunged their comrades into the abyss.

The final words of James Hope, his closest friend, about HenryJoy McCracken were as follows;

" The very perfection of our organisation in Ulster gave treachery the greater scope. When all our leaders deserted us, HenryJoy McCracken stood alone, faithful to the last. He led on the forlorn hope of the cause at Antrim, and brought the Government to terms with all but the leaders. He died rather than prove a traitor to his cause, of which fact I am still a living witness, who shared in all his exertions while he lived, and defy any authentic contradiction of that assertion now or at any future date.20

Dublin from the Phoenix Park 1820.

Henry
Munro

Henry Munro

Henry Munro 1750-1798

Henry Munro was born in Lisburn in the county of Antrim in 1750. His father who was a descendant of Sir Hector Munro, was of Scottish extraction. Henry was an only son but he had two sisters. Munro came from reasonably well off people and he entered the linen business when he completed his education at Lisburn. In 1795 he married Margaret Johnston from Seymore Hill and they had two children. Munro had good business training but he was not much interested in books. He preferred hunting and shooting as a past time. He was grandmaster of the Freemason's Lodge in Lisburn and he was also a member of the Volunteers. He was known to be a kind and generous man and it was this part of his nature which brought him to support the call for Catholic emancipation. And this in turn led him to join the United Irishmen.

It was said of Munro that " his sense of honour would not allow him to take advantage of another's weakness."1 and this may have been his only flaw. Thomas Russell had been appointed Adjutant General for county Down but when the time for the rising came he was in prison. In his absence and unknown to himself, Munro was appointed to replace Russell. Munro had taken no part in the planning of the rebellion and to all accounts was mainly interested in furthering Catholic emancipation by peaceful means. However even before the news of his appointment reached him, Munro had fled his house and was leading the locals in a determined resistance to the murder and persecution being carried on in the area near him. The Orange yeomanry had run amuck and were torturing and flogging the local people without mercy. When he was informed that the leadership had put him in charge of Down he immediately lead his forces towards Saintfield with the intention of leaving a small band there and then to move on to Ballynahinch and make that his headquarters. These were the instructions he had received from McCracken whose plan it was to take the important towns in Down and Antrim and open a road to Wexford, Carlow and . A large body of rebels had assembled in place near Saintfield on the 9th of June. Colonel Stapleton led a force of yeomanry against them from Newtownards. He also had a company of York Fencibles, some cavalry and two pieces of cannon.

The rebels lay in ambush behind a wide hedge along either side of the road. However the ambush was sparked off too soon and only half of the cavalcade were caught in the ambush. A general melee ensued and eventually Colonel Stapleton retired to Comber. The following day he retreated further to Belfast. Meanwhile the rebels were growing in numbers as many other areas joined the insurrection. An attack was made on Portaferry. This was defended by Captain Matthews who held the town for a time but then retreated to Strangford. Also on the 10th the rebels attacked Newtownards which they eventually took when the defenders retreated. All the rebels then converged on Saintfield until Munro had a force of 7000 men at his command.

Munro sent requisitions to all the neighbouring Gentry and farmers for food and provisions for his troops. Large numbers of women came to the field with supplies. Throughout the day and night of the 12th of June Munro drilled his men and instructed his officers. He ordered the men to be given training in the use of the weapons which were available, including cannon and firearms, as most of them had had no previous experience. None of the rebels had uniforms but they came dressed in their Sunday best for the everyday clothes were rags indeed. The majority of the rebels had pikes, about seven feet long, some perfectly straight with a sharp metal point on top, others had hooks on either side for cutting the reins of the cavalry. It was reported that Munro had eight pieces of cannon but these were mounted on ordinary cars which them less effective because they could not be fired accurately.

On the 11th of June Munro despatched a sufficient force to capture Ballynahinch. This they did meeting no resistance as the few troops there fled as they approached. He then placed a strong force at Creevy Rocks to oppose the march of troops from Belfast and to prevent his line of communication with Saintfield and Ballynahinch being cut off. Munro made it his business to occupy the surrounding heights and he stationed a party at Windmill Hill using his best musketeers for an ambush.

On the 12th of June the Kings troops appeared and Munro's men watched their advance as Nugent's men burned all the houses and cabins along the line of their march. The flames could be seen for miles. McCance led the ambush and held the British in check for several hours until, on Munro's instructions he pulled his men back. General Nugent had 3000 trained soldiers who were not going to be held at bay by a few rebels with muskets for very long. Munro then withdrew his men from Ballynahinch and assembled on Endavady Hill. Nugget's troops entered the town and proceeded to burn and loot. By now it was dark and Nugent made no move to attack Munro's forces. About two o' clock in the morning word came that Nugent's troops were drunk and in disarray in the town. All his officers urged him to launch an immediate attack on the town. Munro refused and said that " they must meet their enemy face to face in the light of day and fight like brave men."2

This decision caused dissension in his camp and many of his men deserted, reportedly 700 in one body. All his men knew that they did not have enough ammunition for the battle the next day. On the 13th of June: early in the morning Munro started the battle firing his cannon from the heights above the town. Nugent's troops replied with more accurate fire. One division of the rebels then charged the town while Munro led the remainder of his forces against the main body of Nugent's troops. Munro eventually reached the town centre and ordered a final charge against the town's most entrenched defenders. This charge however failed and the ensuing musket fire scattered the rebels in all directions. The Kings troops retained the town and the rebels reassembled on Endavady. General Nugent reported to Dublin that the rebels had petitioned for a pardon on the 14th of June. In reply he had agreed to accept their submission on condition that Munro and his principle officers were handed over. Munro was arrested in a cabin where he had taken shelter after the battle. Information of his whereabouts was given in Lisburn. He was tried by court-martial, condemned and executed the same day. He was hanged outside his own house where his mother and sister were living. His house and property in Lisburn were completely destroyed by the yeomen and his head was cut off and placed on a spike over the market house in Lisburn where it remained for some months.

Conclusion

It is interesting to note that like McCracken, Munro was a commander by default and had no real opportunity to think out his position. Also like McCracken he left no body of writing behind by which his motives or influences can be judged. There can be little doubt that these men had three other things in common; Humanity, Dignity and Integrity.

Thomas Russell

Thomas Russell

THOMAS RUSSELL
1767-1803

Thomas Russell is famously referred to as "The Man from God knows Where" which indicates that even those who admired him most knew very little about him. Although he trained the players and helped to shape their goals, he himself was absent from the field in 1798. Dublin Castle knew his worth and they were determined to remove him from the fray even before the a single shot was fired.

Thomas Russell was born at Mallow Co. Cork in 1767. His father was a soldier who fought at Dettingen, Fontenoy and Culloden. The family lived for varying periods in Mallow and Durrow before moving to The Royal Hospital Kilmainham. Thomas was still a boy when they came to Dublin in 1778. There is no record of Russell attending school or University and he received his education mostly from his parents and possibly from some of the retired soldiers in the Royal Hospital. Nevertheless, he was competent in Greek and Hebrew and had extensive knowledge in botany, mineralogy, history and poetry. Russell also had a broad knowledge of English literature and had a deep interest in Bible studies. His father was appointed Captain of invalids at the Royal Hospital Kilmainham and this was Russell's home whenever he was in Dublin. In 1783 Thomas joined brother Ambrose in the 52nd Regiment of Foot and they were soon deployed to protect the British interest in India. His brother had already served in a campaign in America where he was slightly injured. Russell spent three years in India where he visited Bombay and Madras. While in India, Russell developed soldiers habits and a soldier's taste for wine women and song. He was involved in several actions while in India and was promoted to Regimental Quartermaster after the siege of Cannanore. However when a peace treaty was signed with the local Sahib, the Regiment was reduced in size and Russell was brought home to Ireland on half pay. Russell arrived back in Dublin in 1787 and spent the next three years living with his family in the Royal Hospital. His income amounted to £28 a year but as he spent most of his time studying he was able to live comfortably on this salary. His political views during this period are not known but when he met Wolfe Tone in the Irish House of Commons in July 1790 he was quick to praise the Whig opposition. Wolfe Tone had a different view. It was probably this disagreement at their very first meeting that sparked off the chemistry that continued to exist between Wolfe Tone and Thomas Russell till the end of their lives. The new acquaintances agreed to meet for dinner the following day and they were practically inseparable for the next three months. Russell was impressed by Tone's wide experience of law and politics both in Dublin and London. Tone was impressed with Russell's military experience and with the depth of his learning on a wide range of topics. Both Tone and Russell regarded the Irish parliament as corrupt and in need of immediate reform. Although anxious for fair play, both were still very much in sympathy with the British Empire. Having spent a pleasant summer by the seaside, in a cottage rented by Wolfe Tone at Irishtown, Thomas Russell set off to take up a new commission in Belfast.

Russell arrived in Belfast in September 1790. He was stationed at the Artillery barracks and being a commissioned officer, he had comfortable quarters and took his meals in the officers mess He quickly became popular among Belfast society, his striking appearance and good manners making him a favourite with the ladies and gentlemen alike. Belfast was a very different place from Dublin. All the power and pomp of the Administration was focused in Dublin, whereas Belfast was firstly a commercial city. The people of Belfast were doers rather then talkers and the city was one of business rather than one of show. Russell's wide range of interests brought him into contact with an ever growing circle of friends and admirers. Much of his time was spent in pubs and clubs but he also met many family men like Neilson, Simms and Sinclair. Russell also met Bunting and McCracken soon after he arrived. Edward Bunting was engaged in the collection of ancient Irish airs for the harp and Russell was among the first to assist and encourage him.

Among the diverse topics that Russell encountered when he went to Belfast, one seemed common to all. The protection of English interests resulted in the people of Belfast being at a grave disadvantage in terms of trade and commerce. The cry in Belfast was first and foremost for free trade. This proposition was promoted most vigorously by the Northern Whig Club. William Sinclair introduced Russell to the Club and he became a member early in 1791. In the wake of the French revolution and the publication of Thomas Paine's " The Rights of Man " the dissenting people of Belfast were consumed with a desire for Parliamentary Reform. The Dublin Parliament had never catered for their needs and the Protestant Ascendancy had accorded the Dissenters little more privileges than those of the Catholics. More and more it was thought that an alliance with the Catholics might serve better the interests of both.

Russell discussed these topics constantly with all the chief opinion formers of Belfast. But not all of his friends were idealists and one of those he trusted, Thomas Digges was a confirmed cynic. Russell learned much from Digges. Digges told Russell the rich could never be trusted and then he borrowed £200 from Russell. When Digges failed to return the money, Russell was forced to sell his commission in order to meet his own debts. As a result Russell was unemployed in Belfast by June 1791. Still a member of the Northern Whig Club he remained in Belfast for the Bastille Day Celebration on the 14th of July. He returned to Dublin on the 17th and remained in residence at the Royal Hospital until the end of the year. In October Russell and Tone set out again to visit their friends in Belfast. They brought with them a proposition for the establishment of a club under the title the United Irishmen. This proposition was championed by Samuel Neilson who on the 14th of October set up a committee with Neilson, William Sinclair, Robert and William Simms, Samuel McTier, Thomas McCabe and William McCleery as its members. On October the 18th a larger meeting took place and twenty eight members approved of the resolutions drafted by Tone and Russell. These called for "complete and radical reform of the representation of people in parliament" and that this reform should include "Irishmen of every religious persuasion" After spending two weeks in Belfast being wined and dined by the leading lights of the city, Russell and Tone returned to Dublin. There they invited James Tandy and Richard McCormick to launch a Dublin branch of the United Irish Club. Neither Russell or Tone attended the first meeting and Simon Butler was appointed Chairman and James Tandy, secretary. Among its members at the outset were William McNevin, Richard McCormick, William Drennan, Thomas Emmet, Oliver Bond, John Sweetman, William James, and Hamilton Rowan. Thomas Russell attended the meetings of the Club regularly which were held in the Music Hall in Fishamble street until he left for Dungannon in January 1792.

Through the good offices of a friend, George Knox who had studied law with Tone in London, Russell was appointed Magistrate in Dungannon in County Tyrone. He took up residence in the town in January '92 but by October he had resigned from this valuable position. The full facts as to why he resigned are not known but he reputedly said;

*" I could not reconcile my conscience to sit as a magistrate on a bench when the practice prevailed of enquiring into a man's religion before inquiring into the crime with which a person is accused."*1

From Dungannon Russell returned to Belfast where he spent some weeks meeting friends and enjoying their hospitality. He had missed the Bastille Day celebration when Tone's new resolutions had been greeted with great enthusiasm. On the 2nd of December Russell left Belfast carrying resolutions from The United Irish Society to the Catholic Convention, which was to meet on the 3rd of December in the Tailor's Hall near Christ Church in Dublin. Russell attended two sittings of the convention and was later present at a number of meetings of the Catholic Committee but his father was dying at this time so he could not give these matters his full attention. John Russell, Thomas's father died on the 5th of December 1792 and was buried in the grounds of the Royal hospital. His Funeral was attended by members of the United Irishmen including Wolfe Tone. Meanwhile an informer in the Dublin society of the United Irishmen, Tom Collins, was giving a full account of the workings of the United Irishmen to Dublin Castle. He drew particular attention to the involvement of Thomas Russell. Russell continued to be an active member of the Dublin Society and worked hard to reform the society during the first half of 1793. Some of the Dublin members were becoming involved in unnecessary public brawls which brought the United Irishmen into disrepute. In March Russell went to Omagh to give evidence in defence of two accused who were subsequently acquitted. He then went to Enniskillen where he made arrangements for his sister Margaret and his two nieces to live there. Russell then returned to Dublin on foot, a journey that took 3 days. In Dublin he was summoned by the House of Lords Select Committee to answer questions about a letter he had received for Wolfe Tone. Thomas Digges had read the letter, made a copy and sent it to Dublin Castle. In the letter Wolfe Tone had discussed several radical ideas and the committee were looking for a more incriminating statement to use against Wolfe Tone. Russell refused to answer any questions implicating Tone. Nevertheless, Lord Fitzgibbon read the letter out in the House of Lords and used it as an excuse to process repressive laws through the Parliament. Simon Butler and Oliver Bond were arrested and held in prison for six months without trial. After he had given evidence before the select committee, Russell and Tone went to the Tailor's Hall to a meeting of the United Irishmen. Russell found that with the increased repression their numbers had now dwindled to less than forty. Russell went to Bodenstown and spent a few days with Wolfe Tone before returning once again to Belfast. Although Russell and Tone spent most of their lives in Dublin, they were always more at home in Belfast.

When Russell arrived back in Belfast he found that Neilson, Simms and Sinclair had been busy and the United Irish Society had grown to tens of thousands of members throughout the north. Moreover with the help Charles Teeling many thousands of Catholics had enrolled in the Society. Samuel Neilson's newspaper " The Northern Star" was eighteen months old and a great success. The paper which had a circulation 4000 copies was widely read throughout the north. The paper gave a full account of the happenings in Dublin, London and Paris. Russell was soon employed to write satirical articles about the aristocracy in Dublin. He particularly criticised Henry Grattan and his Whig party for their failure to mobilise opposition against the Governments new repressive measures. In one of Russell's articles published in the Northern Star on the 30th of August 1793 he wrote the following;

"Mr Pitt by a series of artful manoeuvres had excited a degree of political fanaticism in the people of England, of which history scarce affords an example: any who thought the constitution impaired by lapse of time- that it required repair- any who doubted of its absolute perfection, or defended the French Revolution were considered as detestable political heretics- and pillory's and dungeon's were esteemed punishments too lenient for such crimes. Horrible stories of idealist plots and conspiracies were rumoured and credited: the nation became a nation of spies and informers: and its condition brought to mind the miser in the Comedy, who being robbed and not being able to find the thief, at last caught hold of himself as the aggressor. Mr Grattan, whose fortunes were raised by his country for his exertions on behalf of Liberty, eagerly supported this war against Liberty and lavishly granted the treasure and blood of his countrymen, whose guardian he should have been, for a purpose which they can never approve- let this be joined to the rest of his conduct and then let us think, even himself, whether he would wish that his name should be preserved from oblivion by infamy.2

E   August 30th '93.

These articles were highly popular among the people of the North. Russell spent some time living in the working class homes and began to empathise more and more with the men of no property. The closer he came to the ordinary people the more necessary he thought the need for reform was. Russell spent the month of September in the Mourne mountains where he carried out a geological examinations together with his friend John Templeton. Templeton was at the same time engaged in a botanical survey of the County Down. This gave Russell a further opportunity to meet local people and discover their attitudes to the Government's recent measures. While they were travelling there he visited Ballynahinch, a town that was to be important later. They returned to Belfast journeying all the time on foot and in this way Russell became acquainted with a wide range of people along the way. At the end of November he returned to Dublin and stayed with Wolfe Tone over the Christmas at Bodenstown. Both Russell and Tone attended meetings of the United Irishmen in Dublin during this period also, but the Society was in total disarray. In the middle of January 1794, Russell received news that he had been appointed director of the Belfast Library. His friends John Templeton and Dr. Jim McDonnell had nominated him for the position and they were supported by William Sinclair and Robert Simms. He was guaranteed a salary of £50 a year with a new library premises, his own room and an occasional housekeeper. On January 18th Russell left for Belfast on foot and Wolfe Tone walked with him to the Northside of the Phoenix Park. They were both depressed about the state of the Society in Dublin but ever more optimistic about the growth of the Society in the North. Russell arrived in Belfast and took up his duties as librarian, a job he was well qualified for but he seemed to care little about. He got news of the death of his brother Ambrose in India and this seemed to interfere with his concentration. By August he was back in Dublin to pay another visit to Wolfe Tone. They attended the United Irish Society but nothing had improved. The Government had raided the rooms of the Society in May and as a result membership had dwindled. When Russell returned to Belfast in September '94, he set about re-organising the Society on a more secretive basis. They drafted up a new constitution for the Society and a new organisational structure. HenryJoy McCracken was brought into the organisation in a formal way for the first time. All members in future would be required to take an oath of secrecy. Meanwhile in the first six weeks of 1795 Lord Fitzwilliam had been appointed Viceroy and then withdrawn. His appointment had shown flexibility on the part of the King, as Lord Fitzwilliam was known to favour full Catholic emancipation and also Parliamentary reform. However a few weeks of high hopes were suddenly dashed when he was removed. It was said that he had moved too quickly to implement changes and the Government sacked him. He was replaced by Lord Camden, a singularly vicious man. At the same time Lord Castlereagh was carefully carving out a political career for himself by selling his countrymen into slavery. When Lord Fitzwilliam was recalled both Dublin and Belfast were united in grief. Belfast declared a day of mourning and black flags were hung out of the windows throughout the city. In May of 1795 HenryJoy formally joined the Society and together with Russell and Neilson they began a massive recruitment campaign for the United Irishmen. McCracken and Charles Teeling concentrated their efforts in Antrim and Russell worked in Down, Tyrone and Fermanagh. By the Autumn of '96 there were 90 Clubs across the Province. However, Dublin was still causing problems. Wolfe Tone's Memorandum which was given to Jackson had further compromised the Society. Wolfe Tone was forced to make a deal with the Government and was obliged to leave the country. He arrived in Belfast in May '95 to find the United Irishmen in a magnificent state of readiness. With tens of thousands of members highly politicised, full of confidence and ready for anything. When Tone left Belfast he was seen off by hundreds of cheering supporters. However Belfast had its informers too. Dublin Castle was kept informed about developments in Belfast by men such as John Bird, William Johnston and Rowland O'Connor. Lord Camden instituted a reign of terror and this was supported by Lord Portland. They first concentrated their measures in Connaught where people were flogged and press ganged into the Fleet. Generals Nugent and Lake set about the " pacification " of the populace by means of the pitch-cap and half-hanging. However Lord Castlereagh was less concerned about the Catholics of the South and feared more the Dissenters of the North. On the 16th of September '96 Lord Castlereagh lead a posse into Belfast and commenced a widespread search for the leaders of the United Irishmen. Together with a large contingent of cavalry, he was accompanied by Lord Downshire and Lord Westmeath. They raided the homes of Russell and Neilson and of their friends and they possession of all of Russell's papers from the Belfast Library. Both Neilson and Russell surrendered to the posse under the impression that with a quick trial they would be soon released. This was not to be the case. A further ten of the leading citizens of Belfast were also arrested and they were all taken to Dublin under armed guard. There they were divided into two lots some being held in Newgate prison and the rest held in Kilmainham. Russell was kept in Newgate and Neilson was moved to Kilmainham. McCracken remained at large for a further four weeks until he was arrested in Armagh on the 10th of October. He was lodged with Neilson in Kilmainham. McCracken was held for fourteen months and released in December '97. Neilson was held until February '98 but Russell did not see the outside of prison until 1802.

The prisoners were treated humanely, allowed visitors and could purchase food, clothing and other supplies from outside Meanwhile outside the repression was intensified. Neilson's newspaper was destroyed and the type and printing equipment thrown out on to the streets of Belfast. Every day the prisoners received new stories about hangings, beatings and house-burning. The Catholic members of the United Irishmen suffered the most, as they had no protection under the law. The army, judges and the orange mobs were all ranged against them. But the Presbyterian members of the United Irishmen were also cruelly attacked and many were held on a filthy ship in Belfast dock. Property was confiscated, and businesses destroyed. The Orange order and the Militia were given free rein to act as they pleased and a special law was passed to protect them from prosecution. Catholics hid in the ditches, Presbyterians bolted the doors of their houses and remained indoors. The Government moved Militia's around the country so that their evil deeds would not be known in the area's where they lived. In December Wolfe Tone arrived in Bantry Bay with thirty four ships and twenty thousand French troops. But General Hoche and his ship was lost in the Atlantic and although the ships remained in Bantry for two weeks they never succeeded in effecting a landing.

The arrival of the French Fleet had three separate effects. Firstly, the British switched the repression to wards the south. Secondly, the people began demanding that the rising should take place immediately as a war was already being waged against them. Thirdly, The United Irishmen were in total confusion. Their most capable leaders were in prison or abroad. Thomas Russell was told by the Chief Secretary, in reply to several letters he had written demanding his release, that he would not be released "until the war is over."3 It is thought that Russell had admirers in the Government who wanted to spare him from involvement in the Rebellion which they knew was coming and which they were trying to provoke! In desperation the hopes of the United Irishmen finally rested in the brilliance of one man Lord Edward Fitzgerald. Lord Edward, a brother of the Duke of Leinster was appointed Commander-in-Chief of the United Irish Army. Having had no previous contact with the United Irish leaders he entered Kilmainham Jail in the middle of '97 to confer with Neilson and McCracken. He was unable to visit Russell and Russell only met Lord Edward when he was dying in Newgate in May of '98. Russell became ill on a number of occasions during his long stay in Newgate for despite access to food and clothing, the place was filthy and a constant series of epidemics ran through the prison. The prison Doctor prescribed a half pint of wine a day as a medicine for Russell and this was paid for by the state. He was also free to augment this supply at his own expense as there was no ban on alcohol. The prison Governor often joined Russell for a drink as did many of his visitors, including those carrying letters to him from the Government. Russell's other needs in the way of creature comforts were also satisfied, as prisons were run as a kind of profit making business in those days. Throughout 1797 all the Northern leaders were held in prison. At this time the leaders in Leinster progressed rapidly. Lord Edward and Arthur O'Connor drew up a plan for a rising. They appealed to the French for aid. Wolfe Tone and Edward Lewins continually pressed the French for assistance. By February '98 all the Northern leaders with the exception of Russell had been released. But by March all the leading figures in the Leinster Directory were in prison with the exception of Lord Edward. The French promised to arrive by April. The rising was given the go-ahead for the 23rd of May. Lord Edward was captured on the 19th of May. Russell saw Lord Edward in Newgate on his first night there and expressed the view that Lord Edward died of pneumonia having been brought in with gunshot wounds but also with a heavy cold. The rising went ahead on the 23rd with Kildare, Carlow and Wexford among the first counties to rise. However Neilson was back in prison having been captured trying to organise the escape of the other leaders in

Newgate. HenryJoy McCracken led the United Irishmen into the battle in the North on the 7th of June but by the middle of July all the major fighting had ceased. The Leinster leaders were being brought to trial on high treason. HenryJoy, and many of Russell's other personal friends had by now either been killed in battle or hanged after court-martial. On the 26th of June John and Henry Sheares, John McCann, William Byrne, Oliver Bond and Samuel Neilson were placed on trial for High treason. Neilson then entered into discussions with the Government. He proposed a "pact" whereby all the prisoners would give the Government a full account of their involvement in the United Irishmen in return for charges being dropped and an agreement to emigrate. In return the Government would reprieve Oliver Bond and William Byrne who had already been sentenced to hang. Neilson's position was that the rising had failed and it was better to compromise with the Government and save the people from needless bloodshed. Russell was repulsed by the proposal. He wanted to reserve the right of the people to rise and he knew that Wolfe Tone was still engaged in trying to get the French to invade. However as his own life was not in danger, he could not by default be a party to the deaths of his comrades. Russell knew that signing the pact meant that those who were prepared to carry on the fight were being placed in an impossible position. He feared that the tens of thousands who had been primed to fight, would see the pact, as the leaders selling out to save their own lives. The only redeeming feature of the pact was the clause which said that none of the prisoners would be required to give the names of any of their accomplices. Russell signed but he was never required to give evidence. Statements were given by Neilson, Thomas Emmet, William McNevin and Arthur O'Connor representing the prisoners in Kilmainham, Newgate and the Bridewell. The pact failed to save Byrne who was executed while negotiations were still in progress. Bond was reprieved but died of a heart attack some weeks later. The United Irish leaders gave the Government a detailed account of their plans and their communications with the French. These statements were given early in the month of August. The most extraordinary thing is, that when General Humbert landed at Killala later that same month, the British were, for the first time ever, taken totally by surprise. General Humbert was less than pleased when he heard about the pact. It made it difficult to recruit local support when the people knew that their leaders were soon to emigrate. Russell was embarrassed when English newspapers reported that The United Irish Leaders " had implored mercy." By the time Wolfe Tone sailed for Donegal, the British were well informed and the people were totally disillusioned. When Wolfe Tone was arrested he was held in the Royal Barracks. This is the first time Wolfe Tone had been detained in prison. Russell had been in prison for three years but now they were in different prisons. Russell and Tone had been the closest possible friends but they had not seen each other since May 1795. A pact had been signed to save the lives of the leaders but Wolfe Tone was now on trial for High treason. Russell became frantic to save Wolfe Tone. Having refused to use the goodwill towards him which existed within the Government for his own benefit and having been slow to sign a document to save Byrne and Bond, Russell used every means at his disposal to save Wolfe Tone. He wrote to Peter Burrows, a barrister who agreed to represent Tone and raised money for his defence. He wrote to the prisoners in Kilmainham demanding they reopen negotiations with the Government so that Wolfe Tone could be included in the "pact." Thomas Emmet replied saying that any intervention by the prisoners would only encourage the Government to act more harshly against Wolfe Tone. Wolfe Tone's trial and sentence caused Russell much anger and frustration, but his subsequent suicide left him in the depths of sorrow and despair.

For the next few months the state prisoners were expecting arrangements to be made for their departure to America which was part of the Kilmainham Treaty. However America refused to accept them and eventually in March 1799 they were shipped to Scotland. They left Dublin on the 19th of March on board the "Ashton Smith" and called first at Belfast where they picked the state prisoners from the north. In all twenty prisoners were eventually lodged in Fort George in the northwest of Scotland. The regime at the prison was much more flexible and the prisoners had greater access to fresh air and exercise and they were even allowed to swim in the nearby sea. As their visitors had to travel long distances some of their families were allowed to live in the prison for long periods. Russell enjoyed his stay at Fort George. He kept his journal, read extensively and wrote numerous letters to his sister and brother. He described his Gaoler, Colonel Stuart as a gentleman, polite and humane. The prisoners had ample opportunity to discuss the rebellion and the causes of its failure. Although Robert Simms had walked away from his comrades in June of 98 and Neilson was the architect of the surrender, Russell never blamed them for the failure. But the death of his close friends weighed heavily on Thomas Russell. When the last of the prisoners were released in 1802, he made straight for Paris. There Russell received money sent to him by Robert Simms. In Paris Russell met General Humbert who had led the only French force during the Rebellion which had actually touched land. Russell noticed that Bonaparte's administration was cold towards the Irish. He also felt that Napoleon's imperial ambitions ran counter to the republican ideals which most of the Irish radicals espoused. However in Paris Russell met Robert Emmet who was there to present his plan to Napoleon. This plan provided for a French force to land at Galway and March to Derry. Meanwhile Russell and Emmet bought a warehouse at the port of Le Harve and filled it with cheap arms, surplus from the wars on the continent. From September to march of 1803 Russell continued to ship these arms in small quantities to various ports in Ireland. The arms were generally hidden in tallow barrels and other commercial containers of the time. At the end of March Russell himself returned to Ireland. Together with Robert Emmet, William Hamilton, William Dowdall and Michael Dwyer they all assembled in Rathfarnham to discuss the preparations for a second rising. Robert Emmet was to capture Dublin Castle. Michael Dwyer was to make guerrilla strikes on the city from his base in the Dublin Mountains. Veterans from Carlow and Kildare were to re-organise locally and James Hope and Thomas Russell were to re-activate the forces in the North. Both Russell and Hope made separate trips to the North to gain information on the likelihood of support for a rising there among the people. They reported that if Dublin was captured, Belfast would support the rising also. After three months of planning a final meeting was held in Crow street in Dublin before the three Northern leaders set off for the North at the beginning of July. Russell was to act as General for Antrim and Down, Hamilton was to lead the rebels in County Cavan and James Hope was to act as aid-de-camp to Russell. They first stopped at Newry where a meeting had been planned but nobody turned up. Hope and Russell then went to Knockbracken where they stayed for a few days. Several of their former associates came to visit them including Robert Simms who said that the plan was not feasible, Russell then went to Belfast where he met a lot of his former comrades. Most of them expressed grave doubts about any possibility of success. Russell and Hope then went on a tour of many of the local towns in the County of Antrim. They got very little support and were continually asked if a French invasion could be expected. The only support they could expect was from the poorest Catholics. This made the wealthy Presbyterians even less likely to help. On the 22nd of July Russell held a meeting in Ballynahinch He was assured of between a hundred and two hundred men in Downpatrick. At this meeting Russell explained the details of the plan which he had kept secret up till then. The rising was to commence the following day the 23rd all over Ireland. He said that the French had given £30,000 in support of the Revolution. 20,000 guns were to be landed at Kilkeel. All the Orangemen were to be attacked and their arms taken from them. From Ballynahinch Russell went to Loughinisland where he expected support from the local Catholic population. When he arrived he met the local parish priest who, when he realised Russell's purpose, went about the town warning the people not to get involved. Patrick Lynch who lived in the town and who had been Russell's Irish teacher, spoke to Russell and tried to dissuade him from launching the Rebellion. Russell failed to gather enough support for the rising at Loughinisland. At several other places throughout the north small groups gathered but with numbers few no actions were taken. However Russell's movements had been reported to the authorities by several different sources and he was compelled to return to Belfast and go into hiding. MaryAnn McCracken arranged a hiding place for Russell outside Belfast. The Rebellion in Dublin had been equally futile with premature explosions and Lord Kilwarden being brutally killed with the result that the surprise element of the rising was completely lost. Russell remained in hiding for some weeks until he heard of Emmet's capture. A reward of £1500 was offered for the capture of Thomas Russell, with some of his former friends putting up some of the money. However he was not betrayed by the people and with the help of MaryAnn McCracken he travelled to Drogheda from where he made his way to Dublin with intention of rescuing Robert Emmet. He first found shelter in Blackrock but later spent some time hiding in the Liberties. On the 7th of September he took lodgings at 29 Parliament street. Robert Emmet was at this time held in Kilmainham jail. Russell posed as a "Mr. Harris " and booked three rooms for a week saying Mrs. Harris would join him in a few days. The Lodgings were owned by a Mr Muley and an agreement was made whereby Mr Harris would have his meals and newspapers brought to his room. After two days a neighbour, Watty Cox, remarked to his friend John Emerson that there was a guest at Muley's who remained indoors at all times and had his meals brought to his room. Emerson having satisfied himself that something was suspicious, reported this to Dublin Castle. Major Sirr, who had been out all day collecting evidence against Robert Emmet, was less than pleased to be sent out again on what he considered a false alarm. He entered the room of Thomas Russell at 9.30pm on the 9th of September 1803. Within five minutes Thomas Russell was a prisoner in Dublin Castle. The authorities in Dublin Castle were swamped with letters of congratulation when Russell was apprehended. The Loyalists of Belfast wanted him tried and executed in Belfast. Russell was held in Kilmainham from the 10th of September until the 12th of October. While there attempts were made to obtain information from him by various different means. The Government wanted to know what connections existed between the rebels in Ireland and conspirators in England and the French. Besides being interrogated by Government officials Russell was interviewed by Leonard McNally who had been in the pay of the British since 1795, but who was still posing as a sympathiser with the United Irishmen. Russell may have suspected McNally for he revealed nothing that the Government did not already know. In the meantime Robert Emmet was brought from Kilmainham to Green Street, tried, convicted and returned to Kilmainham on the 19th of September. On the 20th he was taken out again and brought to Thomas Street where he was executed, his body being returned again to Kilmainham. These events must have pressed heavily on Russell who was in constant communication with senior officials at the jail. The prison chaplain persuaded Russell to make a religious confession which he then conveyed to the Government. In his confession Russell says;

" *In the awful Presence of God and at his Holy Table I acknowledge myself to have been guilty of many immoral acts, many impieties and negligence of Sacred Duties, but as to political opinions and political actions I have ever been led by what reason, the result of deep meditation and laboured reflection have shown me to be right. I never intended, by what I have politically done, anything, other than to advantage of my fellow creatures and even the happiness of my adversaries. Whether the Lord shall be pleased to extend my life for forty years or to cut my thread of existence in an hour, I shall not cease from the work I have begun nor give it up but with life itself.*"4

Dublin Castle decided to have Russell tried at Downpatrick because of " the magnitude of his treason and the strong desire expressed by several gentlemen of the North to have him tried where his execution would have greatest effect," On the 12th of October Russell was moved to Downpatrick under a heavily armed escort. On the 20th he appeared before the special commission charged with High treason. The presiding Judge was Baron George and the prosecutor was Standish O 'Grady who had already acted against Emmet. Russell was represented by Henry Joy a cousin of HenryJoy. The McCracken family, most notably MaryAnn put all their resources at Russell's disposal in an effort to have him acquitted or even to bribe officials to allow him escape. At the trial evidence was given against Russell by William Cosby, Henry Smith, James Fitzgerald and Fr. McCarton. There were no witnesses for the defence. Henry Joy questioned the jurisdiction of the court saying that no overt Rebellion had taken place in County Down. This was over-ruled by the Judge. The Judge charged the jury and after a short interval they returned a verdict of guilty. Russell then addressed the court. He said he had no regrets about his political involvement of the last thirteen years. He asked that he might be the only one who would fall and he insisted that the other prisoners had been induced to join in a business that did not originate with themselves. Finally Russell said;

*"politically I have done nothing but what I glory in, morally I acknowledge myself a grievous sinner. I trust for pardon and mercy through my saviour as I do most sincerely forgive all who are about to take my life."*5

Thomas Russell was hanged on 21st of October 1803 in front of Downpatrick Jail. His body was buried in the cemetery of the local Church. MaryAnn McCracken had a simple memorial erected over his grave with an inscription bearing the words;

" The Grave of Russell"

end

The execution of Robert Emmet 1803.

Robert Emmet

Robert Emmet

Robert Emmet
1778-1803

*" Liberty is the child of Oppression and the birth of the offspring
is the death of the parent: While Tyranny, like the bird of the
desert, is consumed in flames ignited by itself, and the whole of
it's existence is spent providing the means of self destruction. "* 1
Robert Emmet 1802

Robert Emmet was the youngest son of Dr. Robert Emmet and a
brother of Thomas Emmet. He was born in Dublin in1778 and he
attended schools in Bride Street, Grafton Street and later at
Camden Street. He entered Trinity at fifteen years of age in 1793.
His main interest was chemistry and is reputed to have nearly
poisoned himself while mixing chemicals in amateur
experiments at his home. He was expelled from Trinity in 1798
for refusing to answer questions on oath about the United
Irishmen. He visited his brother in 1800 and stayed for some time
with the State prisoners at Fort George in Scotland. It is thought
that his subsequent visit to the Continent involved him in
carrying messages to the United Irishmen in Paris. He also
visited Switzerland, Austria, Holland and Spain on that occasion.
He returned to Paris to meet his brother Thomas who was just
released from Fort George in July 1802. He also met Thomas
Russell and together the Irish émigrés discussed the situation of
their home country. Robert Emmet met with Napoleon and
Tallyrand and formed the opinion that the French were only
interested in Ireland, as a diversionary tactic to assist the
invasion of Britain. However Robert Emmet had received
invitations from persons in high office in Dublin to mount
another insurrection in Ireland. He was promised huge sums of
money to finance the Rebellion and he was supplied with
accurate information about the internal workings of Dublin
Castle. Emmet was given good reason to believe that many
thousands of the survivors of the '98 Rebellion were ready and

willing to resume the fight at a time when circumstances were right.

Emmet and Russell bought a warehouse at the port of Le Harve and they filled it with arms which they bought on the Continent, with money supplied by the French. From September 1802 until March 1803 the arms were shipped to Ireland by various carriers on regular commercial sailings. The arms were concealed in paint and tallow barrels and were landed in Dublin without suspicion. Emmet returned to Ireland in October 1802 leaving Russell to carry on shipping the remaining arms. When he arrived back in Ireland Emmet took lodgings in Harold's Cross where he used the alias Robert Hewit. He also had a house in Butterfield Lane, near Rathfarnham where he went under the alias Robert Ellis. In this house he had a portion of the wall hollowed out so that he could conceal himself if the house was raided. Emmet met with the veterans of '98 to seek their support for his coming revolt. He also had a meeting with John Keogh who lived nearby at Harold's Cross. Russell arrived from the Continent in March and Emmet and Russell then intensified their preparations. They recruited new support and Emmet's personal staff included James Hope, Barry Duggan, William Dowdall, Michael Quigley and William Hamilton. Both Hope and Russell made visits to the north to assess the level of support that could be anticipated. They already had promises of support from Wicklow, Wexford and Kildare. Robert Emmet held a major meeting at his house in Rathfarnham. Among those who attended was the celebrated guerrilla leader Michael Dwyer who had remained at large and harried the British successfully since 1798. Emmet set out his plan. He would first take Dublin Castle. This could be done with a small number of men. The principle officers of Dublin Castle would be held hostage. They would then storm the arms stores at the Pigeon House and when this was taken, rockets would be fired which would signal that the revolt had begun. The Kildare men would come to Dublin the day before and assemble at varying points near Dublin Castle. Russell, Hamilton and Hope would go north and start the rebellion on the 23rd of July. Emmet had established arms depots at Patrick's street, Thomas street and Marshalsea Lane. In one depot gunpowder and rockets were being manufactured. In the second timber was being sawn to make pikes. In the third, arms and pikes were being stored. Michael Dwyer agreed to lead 500 men in from the mountains to create distractions and disturbances in the south of the city, conditional on the rockets going off. On the 14th of July, the anniversary of the French Revolution was celebrated in Dublin with bonfires throughout the city. This was the first time since 1798 that the people had shown any spirit. Although the city was rife with rumours of a rising, the Government had no firm information about it. Many thousands had agreed to take part in the rising but the ordinary people were so repulsed by the actions of the police during '98 that even those who would like to inform, were afraid to talk to the police. None of those who were involved with Emmet in the manufacture of the arms at the various depots gave information to the Government prior to the revolt. This was surprising since at least forty men were involved in their manufacture. On the day before the rising an item was dropped on the ground and it could not be found " because there were too many people in the building." Robert Emmet spent his personal fortune purchasing equipment and materials for the rising. He had money given to him by secret sources, but much of the money he was promised never materialised. Michael McDaniel was making rockets in the Patrick's street depot on the 16th of July when, being drunk, he accidentally set off an explosion injuring two of Emmet's men seriously. The depot was quickly evacuated, and Emmet's men removed every trace of explosive so that when major Sirr examined the premises he thought the explosion must have been caused by natural gas. Emmet's men salvaged all the arms, fuses and rockets which were undamaged. However Emmet decided to quit his lodgings and spent the remaining weeks living in the Marshalsea depot, which was just off Thomas street. After the explosion some of Emmet's supporters wanted him to defer the revolt. Emmet refused to defer it because word had already been sent to his comrades in other counties and he was of the opinion that the longer it was deferred, the more likely it was that the British would discover their plans. Moreover, large numbers of Wicklow men and Wexford men were in Dublin for seasonal work and if they returned home they would not be available to assist in the revolt. In the days before the rising, Emmet slept on a mattress on the floor of the depot in Marshalsea Lane, surrounded by arms and ammunition. In this depot alone he has 45lbs of cannon powder, eleven boxes of gunpowder, sixty thousand musket balls, numerous rockets and two hundred and fifty six hand-grenades. He also had twenty thousand pikes. Emmet was fully aware that in the '98 Rebellion, pikes were useless when the rebels were attacked with cannon and muskets. On the 23rd of July he sent McDaniel out to collect a consignment of pistols and muskets which he had previously ordered. He gave McDaniel 60 guineas to pay for the arms but McDaniel disappeared with the money and from that moment things went badly wrong for Emmet. Emmet then met with the Kildare leaders in the White Bull Inn in Thomas street at 2pm. They demanded to be shown the arms which they needed for their front ranks. Due to McDaniel's action the Kildare leaders decided that the revolt was hopeless and ordered their men to return home. Michael Dwyer would not commit his men until the Castle was taken. On the evening of the 22nd it was planned to kidnap the Commander-in Chief of the British forces. He lived in the Royal Hospital at Kilmainham and he took a walk every evening along the South Circular road. The plan was that a number of men would pose as Sheriff's officers and arrest him with a forged Writ, and take him by force to Emmet's quarters. The plan was called off when some of Emmet's officers got cold feet at the last moment. Emmet had a constant stream of visitors at his depot from all parts of the country and he was still confident of success. However two men living at Chapelizod, Clarke and Wilcock, noticed large numbers of men passing through from Kildare. They set off on horseback for the city and informed the authorities in Dublin Castle. In the meantime Henry Howley, who was bringing Robert Emmet's coach across Queen's Bridge, got himself involved in an unnecessary fight with Colonel Brown. When Brown drew his sword, Howley shot him with his pistol and then fled leaving Emmet's coach unattended. Emmet's plan was to enter the Castle in two coaches, first by deception and then by force. He had sufficient armed men ready for this purpose, but Howley was in charge of procuring the coaches. Emmet's plan was to kidnap the Viceroy and keep him and his family hostage. They had hundreds of local people ready to pour into the Castle when possession of it was gained. Emmet had obtained special liveries so that the coach drivers could pass through the Castle gates unmolested. By this time hundreds of Emmet's supporters had gathered in Thomas Street and the surrounding area's. They were all waiting for his signal. Emmet was still prepared to defer his action until he could get replacement coaches and enter the Castle. But Michael Quigley raised the alarm saying that a troop of soldiers was coming to capture the warehouse. Emmet decided to start the revolt rather than lose all the arms and be captured like rats in the warehouse. The crowds were brought into the depots and a large body was quickly armed. A despatch rider was seen riding along the quays with information for the Commander-in Chief. Emmet had posted lookouts to watch for this and the rider was quickly shot. Emmet sent men to block the entry to the city at Islandbridge and to cut off the Royal Barracks and the Royal Hospital. At 9pm. Emmet lead his forces out the depot and into Thomas Street. They paraded down the street with swords drawn and pistols firing. They were supported by a large body of local people not all of whom were sober. Some of those who had taken pikes and fire arms began to attack local premises and engaged in looting. Lord Kilwarden who arrived in Thomas street at about this time came upon the parade from behind. When some of the mob saw him they turned on him and attacked his carriage. Emmet and those at the front of the march were unaware of what was happening at the rear. By the time Emmet and the other leaders returned, Lord Kilwarden was already fatally wounded. In all this confusion Emmet abandoned any hope of capturing the Castle. He tried in vain to quell the riots until in the end he and his closest followers retreated down Francis's street and made their way to the Dublin mountains. Emmet was shocked and disgusted with the failure of many to turn out, and even more disgusted by the behaviour of many who did. Although advised that the Wicklow men and Wexford men were still willing to rise, Emmet ordered an end to all hostilities. Emmet was perfectly safe in Wicklow mountains which had sheltered Michael Dwyer for five years. He was offered safe passage out of the country by means of the fishing boats on the nearby coast. However Emmet did not want to leave Ireland without seeing his girlfriend Sarah Curran. He returned to his old lodgings at Harold's Cross and wrote several letters in the hope of meeting with her. Emmet remained at large for four weeks after the rising. While waiting for a reply to his letters he was arrested at 7pm. on the evening of the 25th of A August 1803. He was taken by Major Sirr, who claimed that he did not know what Emmet looked like until after he had arrested him. Emmet was taken to the Castle were he was questioned for a short time before being moved to Kilmainham. Robert Emmet was tried for High Treason under a special commission at Green Street on Monday the 19th of September 1803. There were three Judges, Lord Norbury, Mr. George, and Mr. Daly. The prosecutor was the Attorney General Mr. Standish O'Grady. Addressing the Jury O'Grady said ;

" Upon former occasions, persons were brought to the bar of this court, implicated in rebellion in various though inferior degrees. On this occasion we have brought to the bar of justice, not a person who had been seduced by others, but a gentleman to whom the Rebellion may traced as the origin, the life and soul of it. Sometime before Christmas the prisoner who had visited several countries including France, returned to this country full of mischievous designs which have been fully exposed. He persevered in fermenting a rebellion which does not complain of any existing grievances, which does not flow from any immediate oppression and which is not pretended to have been provoked by our mild and gracious King or by the administration employed by Him to execute His authority. It is a rebellion which avows itself to come, not to remove any evil which the people feel, but to recall the memory of grievances which, if they ever existed, must have long since passed away. "

Finishing up his case O'Grady said;

*" Gentlemen, you have the life of a fellow subject in your hands, and by the peculiar benignity of our laws he is presumed to be an innocent man until your verdict shall find him guilty. If upon the evidence you shall be so satisfied that this man is guilty, you must discharge your duty to your King, your country and your God. If, on the other hand nothing shall appear sufficient to affect him, we shall acknowledge that we have grievously offended him, and will heartily participate in the common joy that must result from the acquittal of an innocent man. "*2

Seventeen witnesses gave evidence against Robert Emmet including Joseph Rawlins. Michael Frayne, John Fleming,

Terence Colgan, Patrick Farrell, Sergeant Rice, Colonel Vassal, Frederick Darley, Captain Evelyn, Robert Linsay and Major Sirr. After all the evidence had been heard, Lord Norbury instructed the jury and reviewed the whole of the evidence and explained to them the law. The jury without leaving the box, pronounced the prisoner guilty. The Judge then asked Emmet "what he had to say, why judgement of death and execution should not be passed against him." Robert Emmet then made a speech from the dock as follows;

" My lords I am asked what I have to say, why sentence of death should not be passed against me according to the law? I have nothing to say that can alter your pre-determination, nor that it will become me to say, with any view to the mitigation of the sentence which you are to pronounce and I must abide by. But I have much to say, of something which interests me more than life, and which you have laboured to destroy. I have much to say, why my reputation should be rescued from the load of false accusations and calumny which has been cast upon it. I do not imagine that seated where you are, your mind can be so free from impurity as to receive the least impression from what I am going to utter. I have no hopes that I can anchor my character in the breast of a court constituted and trammelled as this is. I only wish, and this is the utmost that I expect, that your Lordships may suffer it to float down your memories untainted by the foul breath of prejudice, until it finds some more hospitable harbour, to shelter it from the storms by which it is buffeted. Was I only to suffer death, after being adjudged guilty by your tribunal, I should bow in silence and meet the fate that awaits me without murmur: but the sentence of the Law that delivers my body to the executioner, will, through the ministry of the law, labour in its own vindication, to consign my character to obloquy: for there must be guilt somewhere, whether in the sentence of the court or in the catastrophe, most determine. A man in my situation has not only to encounter the difficulties of fortune, but the difficulties established by prejudice. The man dies but his memory lives. That mine may not perish, that it may live in the respect of my countrymen, I seize upon this opportunity to vindicate myself from some of the charges laid against me. I appeal to the Immaculate God, I swear by the Throne of Heaven-

before which I must shortly appear- by the blood the men born patriots who have gone before- that my conduct has been, through all this period and through all my purposes, governed only by the conviction which I have uttered, and by not other view than that of their cure, and the emancipation of their country from the superinhuman oppression under which she has long and too patiently travailed: and that I confidently hope that, wild and chimerial as it may appear, there is still union and strength in Ireland to accomplish this noblest of enterprises."

Lord Norbury interrupted Emmet several times during his speech. Emmet addressed the judges thus before carrying on with his speech.

" Why do your Lordships insult me?" Why insult justice in demanding of me "why sentence should not be passed against me"? " - " I know my Lords that form prescribes that you ask that question- the form also presents the right of answering. This no doubt may be dispensed with, and so might the whole ceremony of the trial, since sentence was already pronounced at the Castle before the jury was empanelled. Your Lordships are but the Priest of the Oracle, and I insist on the whole of the forms!"---- " I am charged with being an emissary of France. An emissary of FRANCE! and to what end? Was it for a change of master? Were the French to come as invaders or enemies, uninvited, I would oppose them with the utmost of my strength."

Lord Norbury continued to interrupt but Emmet continued.

" Let no man dare when I am dead to charge me with dishonour! Let no man attaint my memory, by believing that I could have engaged in any cause but that of my country's liberty and independence: or that I could have become the pliant minion of power in the oppression or miseries of my country."

Lord Norbury interrupted again. Emmet addressed him directly.

" My lord, you are impatient for the sacrifice. The blood which you seek is not congealed by the artificial terrors which surround your victim- it circulates warmly and unruffled through the channels which God created for noble purposes, but which you are now bent to destroy, for purposes so grievous, that they cry out to heaven- be yet patient. I have but few words more to say- I am going to my cold and silent grave, my lamp of life is nearly extinguished- my race is run- the grave opens to receive me, and I sink into its bosom. I have but one request to ask at my

*departure from this world, it is - the charity of its silence. Let no man write my epitaph; for as no man who knows my motives dare now vindicate them, let no prejudice or ignorance asperse them. Let them and me rest in obscurity and peace: and my memory in oblivion, until other times and other men can do justice to my character- when my country takes its place among the Nations of the Earth, then, and not until then, let my epitaph be written! I have done. "*3

The trial of Robert Emmet lasted thirteen hours. There was no interval and throughout the day he received no refreshments. He was brought to Newgate at 11 o'clock at night and sentenced to be hanged the next day. Two hours after he arrived, at 1 am. he was moved again to Kilmainham. At ten o'clock the next morning he was visited by Leonard McNally and the Rev. Dr. Gamble. When Emmet asked about his mother McNally informed him that she had died two days earlier. On the night before his execution Emmet wrote a letter to his brother Thomas, who was living in Paris, in which he described in great detail all his plans and preparations for the revolt. He gave it to the Jail Doctor who promised its safe delivery but instead it went straight to Dublin Castle. At 1 p.m. on the 20th Robert Emmet was taken out of Kilmainham and brought to Thomas Street. By all the accounts of those who witnessed his journey, Emmet seemed ignorant of fear. When he reached the scaffold his arms were tied and he was assisted to climb the steps by the executioner, but he mounted the steps quickly and with apparent ease. He addressed the crowd but spoke only to his friends and supporters who were gathered nearest to the platform. He made no reference to political matters. He said "my friends I die in peace and with sentiments of universal love and kindness to all men." He shook hands with some of those on the platform and gave his watch to the executioner. The rope was placed about his neck and a black cap pulled down over his face. He was hanged and after being left to hang for a prescribed time, his remains were taken down and his head cut off and held up by the hair and paraded along the front of the platform the executioner proclaiming " this is the head of the traitor Robert Emmet."   Robert Emmet expected an attempt to be made to rescue him from the gallows. Thomas Russell had come back to Dublin with the intention of making such an attempt but he was captured himself on the 19th of

August in Parliament street. Emmet's body was removed by common cart and brought back to Kilmainham jail where it was kept until arrangements were made for its burial. After some hours it was eventually buried beside the grave of Felix Rourke, the Wicklow rebel, at the right hand corner of the burying ground and a short distance from the old entrance to Bully's Acre in the grounds of the Royal Hospital Kilmainham.

end

Thomas Emmet
1764-1827

Thomas Emmet was born in Cork in 1764. He entered Trinity in 1781. He then moved to Edinburgh where he obtained degrees in Medicine. He returned to Trinity where he studied Law and was called to the Bar in 1790. He represented Napper Tandy in a famous case against Lord Westmoreland. He joined the United Irishmen in 1795. He was one of those who wanted the rebellion postponed until French assistance arrived. He was arrested at Oliver Bond's house on the 12 of March 1798 along with the other members of the Leinster Directory. He gave evidence to the select committee as part of the Kilmainham Treaty. He was transported to Fort George where he remained until his release in 1802. He then went to Holland where he stayed for two years. In 1804 he went to America where he returned to the practice of law. He died in1827 and is buried at St. Mark's in Broadway New York.

Oliver Bond
1760-1798

Oliver Bond was born in Ulster in 1760. He was the son of a wealthy Presbyterian minister. Oliver Bond moved to Dublin and set up a very successful woollen business and as a result made a large fortune. He was one of the first to join the United Irishmen when it was set up and he became secretary in 1793. He was one of its most energetic supporters and he issued promissory notes to the poor of Dublin which would be redeemable in the event of a Republic being set up. His wife carried a bible around so she could swear women into the United Irishmen. She also smuggled newspapers and writing materials into Kilmainham Jail in a pie she baked for Christmas 1796. Oliver Bond, in conjunction with Simon Butler published a proclamation condemning the Government's Select Committee as illegal and unconstitutional in 1793. They were both promptly imprisoned, fined £500 each and held for six months without trial. Oliver Bond was a member of the Northern Directory of the United Irishmen and also a member of the Leinster Directory. Thomas Reynolds, who was also a member of the Leinster Directory, gave information to Dublin Castle which led to a raid on Oliver Bond's house on the 12th of March 1798. Bond was arrested along with all the other members of the Directory who were meeting there. He was charged with High Treason, convicted and sentenced to death but was reprieved as part of the Kilmainham treaty. However he died of a heart attack some weeks after the trial and is buried in St. Michan's Churchyard in Church street.

Simon Butler

Simon Butler was the first President of the United Irishmen in Dublin, a position to which he was elected on the 9th of November 1791. He published a list of the anti-popery laws which was a great help to the Catholic Convention. He was summoned before the Select committee in 1793 and imprisoned for six months. The United Irish Society gave a dinner in his honour in Newgate Prison and the Catholic Committee gave him an engraved silver plate. He was struck off the List of King's Council in 1793. He died in 1797.

William McNevin
1763-1841

William McNevin was born in Galway in 1763. He was a nephew of Baron McNevin of Bohemia and he lived with his uncle in Prague for some years while he was studying. He received a Degree in Medicine in Austria in 1783 and then returned to Dublin where he set up practice. He was a leading member of the Catholic Committee. He was invited by Lord Edward to join the United Irishmen in 1797. He joined Edward Lewins in Paris in 1797 in an effort to get French support for the rebellion. He returned to Ireland in 1798, and was mainly responsible for the postponement of the Rebellion. He was arrested at Oliver Bond's house along with the other members of the Leinster Directory. He gave evidence as part of the Kilmainham treaty and was transported to Fort George where he remained until 1802. In 1803 he joined the French army but resigned after two years. In 1805 he went to New York were he returned to the practice of medicine. He was a Professor of Chemistry in the College of Physicians and was made Inspector of Hospitals in New York in 1822. He died in 1841 and was buried at Long Island New York

Arthur O'Connor
1763-1852

Arthur O'Connor was born in July 1763 in Mitchelstown Co. Cork. He entered Trinity in 1779 and was called to the Bar in 1788 but he never practised law. His uncle, Viscount Longuille procured a seat for him in the Irish House of Commons in 1790 where he joined Lord Edward Fitzgerald. O'Connor was fascinated by the French Revolution and he sympathised with the Catholic cause. He made an important speech in the House on the 4th of July 1795 and thereafter, resigned his seat. He joined the United Irishmen in 1796 along with Lord Edward. In 1797 he set up the "The Press", a republican newspaper which put forward the views of the United Irishmen and gave detailed reports of the happenings in France. In the Spring of 1798 he was sent to Paris by Lord Edward to get French help for the rising but was arrested at Margate along with Fr. Quigley. He was tried for High Treason but acquitted for lack of evidence. He was however taken to Dublin and held in the Bridewell throughout the remainder of 1798. He gave evidence as part of the Kilmainham Treaty and was transported to Fort George along with the other state prisoners. After his release he went to France where he wrote numerous books and was accorded great respect by the French. He died in 1852.

References in Text

Chapter 1

1   Madden , Antrim and Down '98 p.153
2   ibid p.88
3   ibid p.92
4   ibid p.102
5   ibid p.141
6   Latimer, Ulster Biographies, p. 61

Chapter 2

1   Northern Star, 4,1,1792 p.1
2   Madden lives Vol.4 , 4th series p.121-122
3   Madden lives Vol. 1, 2nd series p.265-266
4   ibid p.298
5   Fitzpatrick, The informers of '98, p.114

Chapter 3

1   Madden lives Vol. 2, 2nd series p.375
2   ibid p.380
3   ibid p.421
4   ibid p.422
5   Fitzpatrick, The Informers of '98 p.114
6   ibid p.190

Chapter 4

1   Madden lives Vol. 2, 2nd series p.27
2   ibid p.54
3   ibid p.126-128
4   ibid p.7

Chapter 5
1 Joy Henry, Historical Collections, p.365
2 Madden , Antrim and Down '98, p.102
3 McCracken Letters
4 Madden lives Vol. 2, 2nd series p. 407
5 McCracken Letters
6 ibid
7 Madden lives Vol. 2, 2nd series p.395
8 ibid
9 ibid
10 ibid p.396
11 ibid
12 Madden, Anrtim and Down '98, p.70
13 ibid p.83
14 ibid p.84
15 ibid p72
16 McCracken Letters
17 Madden lives Vol. 2, 2nd series p.495
18 ibid p.496
19 The freeman's Journal 19th July 1798
20 Madden, Antrim and Down '98 p.127

Chapter 6
1 Madden, Antrim and Down p.228

Chapter 7

1 Madden, lives Vol. 2, 3rd series p.155
2 Northern Star 30th Aug. 1793
3 TCD Ms 873/655
4 SPO 620/50/21
5 TCD Ms 873/626

Chapter 8

1 Madden, lives Vol. 2, 3rd series p.301
2 ibid p.443
3 ibid p.450-455

Bibliography

Belfast Newsletter, files in Linnenhall library
Benn George, History of Belfast
Carroll, D., The Man From God Knows Where
Castlereagh, Viscount, Memoirs ed.C Vane
Clifford, B., Thomas Russell and Belfast
Cornwallis, Charles. Diary and Correspondence
Cronin, S., A man of the people- Jimmy Hope
Curtis, E ., A History of Ireland
Dickson, Charles., Revolt in the North
Drennen Letters, Public Record Office, N.Ireland
Elliott, Marianne, Wolfe Tone, Prophet of Irish Independence
Fitzhenry, E., Henry Joy McCracken
Freeman's Journal ,1790-1798 files in National Library of Ireland
Heatley, F. Henry Joy McCracken and His Times
Historical Collections relating to the Town of Belfast 1817
Joy MSS. Linenhall Library
Latimer, W.T. ,Ulster Biographies
Landreth, H., The Pursuit of Robert Emmet
Lecky, W.E., History of Ireland in the Eighteenth Century
McCracken Letters T.C.D.
McNeill, Mary., The Life and Times of MaryAnn McCracken
Madden, R.R. The United Irishmen Their Lives and Times
Madden, R.R. Antrim and Down '98
Madden Papers T.C.D.
MacDermot, F. Theobald Wolfe Tone
McSkimin, The Annals of Ulster
Northern Star ,1792-1997 files in Linnenhall Library
O' Broin, Leon The Unfortunate Mr. Emmet
Owen, D.J., History of Belfast.
Paine, Thomas., The Rights of Man
Press,The.,1796-1798, files in The National library of Ireland.
Teeling, C.H., History of the Irish Rebellion
Tone, T.W. Life Of, by William Tone - Washington,1826
Young, R.M., Ulster in '98

Index

The Song Of Henry Joy
(Traditional)

An Ulster man I'm proud to be
From the Antrim glens I come
Although I labour by the sea
I've followed flag and drum
I heard the martial tramp of men
I've seen them fight and die
Ah well do I remember when
I followed Henry Joy.

I pulled my boat up from the sea
I hid my sails away
I hung my nets on a greenwood tree
And I scanned the moonlit bay
The boys were out, the redcoats too
I kissed my wife goodbye
And in the shade of the greenwood glade
I followed Henry Joy

In Antrim town the tyrant stood
He tore our ranks with ball
But with a cheer and a pike to clear
We swept him over the wall
Our pikes and sabres flashed that day
We won, but lost, ah why?
No matter lads, I fought beside
And shielded Henry Joy

Ah boys, for Ireland's cause we fought,
For her and home we bled
Though our pikes were few our hearts beat true,
And five to one lay dead,
And many a lassie mourned her lad,
And mother mourned her boy;
For youth was strong in the gallant throng
Who followed Henry Joy

The Battles of 1798

Battle	County	Date
Baltinglass	Wicklow	24th May
Ballymore Eustace	Wicklow	24th May
Prosperous	Kildare	24th May
Clane	Kildare	24th May
Kilcullen	Kildare	24th May
Monasterven	Kildare	24th May
Carlow	Carlow	24th May
Dunboyne	Meath	24th May
Dunlavin	Meath	25th May
Tara	Meath	26th May
Kilthomas	Mayo	27th May
Oulart	Wexford	27th May
Enniscorthy	Wexford	28th May
Rathangan	Kildare	29th May
Three Rock Mountain	Wicklow	29th May
The Curragh	Kildare	31st May
Newtownmountkennedy	Wicklow	31st May
Newtownbarry	Wexford	1st June
Gorey	Wexford	4th June
New Ross	Wexford	5th June
Randlestown	Antrim	7th June
Antrim	Antrim	7th June
Saintfield	Down	9th June
Arklow	Wicklow	9th June
Portaferry	Down	11th June
Ballinhinch	Down	12th June
Kilbeggin	Westmeath	15th June
Ballynacarthy	Cork	19th June
Ovitstown	Kildare	19th June
Goffs Bridge	Wexford	20th June
Vinegar Hill	Wexford	21th June
Newbridge	Kildare	23rd June
Castlecomer	Kilkenny	24th June
Hacketstown	Carlow	25th June
Fox's Hill	Meath	29th June
Carnew	Wicklow	1st July
Killala	Mayo	22nd Aug.
Castlebar	Mayo	27th Aug.
Cloony	Sligo	5th Sept.
Granard	Longford	5th Sept.
Ballinamuck	Mayo	8th Sept.
Castlebar	Mayo	12th Sept.
Killala	Mayo	23rd Sept.